DIRTY HERO

A REAPER ROMANCE

STELLA ANDREWS

Copyrighted Material
Copyright © Stella Andrews 2021
Stella Andrews has asserted her rights under the Copyright, Designs and Patents Act 1988 to be identified as the Author of this work. This book is a work of fiction and except in the case of historical fact, any resemblance to actual persons, living or dead, is purely coincidental. All rights reserved. No part of this book may be reproduced or transmitted in any form without written permission of the author, except by a reviewer who may quote brief passages for review purposes only.

18+ This book is for Adults only. If you are easily shocked and not a fan of sexual content then move away now.

18+

NEWSLETTER

Sign up to my newsletter and download a free book

stellaandrews.com

DIRTY HERO

STELLA ANDREWS

He saved me, but who will save me from him?

They call him Snake; I call him a bad day at the office.
A man of extremes. Hard. Ruthless. Dominant.
Dangerous & predatory.
A man of duty and yet a renegade.

I stepped from one nightmare into another and he holds the key to my prison.
I was operating undercover. Then he arrived and everything changed.
Locked in a cabin away from civilization, I am stuck with him until he says otherwise.
An operation gone badly wrong that will take a miracle to put right.
I may have lost everything. My job, almost my life and now my principles because one look at him changes the rules.
He only wants one thing - *me* and is prepared to wait for as long as that takes.

I've never been one to run away from a fight, and something tells me this one is destiny or destruction.

Will it be mine, or his?

If you love a hard, tough alpha male with a soft spot for a beautiful damsel in distress, then this book is for you.

This is an intriguing, emotional and engrossing MC romance filled with thrilling moments, suspense, family, angst and really sexy and steamy scenes.

A must read if you like rough, dirty, tough and sinfully delicious bikers and the women they love.

CHAPTER 1

BONNIE

There's something different in the air tonight. An underlying current of tension that tastes like death. It's all around me, and I breathe it in, knowing there is no escaping it.

As it coats my soul, it weakens me; takes my usual bravery, and neutralizes it in a matter of seconds. I want to run, to hide, anything but face the storm that's building, approaching, waiting to devastate, injure, maim and kill.

"Beer, baby."

Looking up, I stare into the pit of hell. Two deep pools of smoking danger belonging to a man who is fast running out of patience. Defined by violence and outlined in rage.

I just nod and turn away, desperate to break eye contact in the hope it will save me from a fate worse than death. Him.

They call him Blaze; I call him the devil. Every night terror I've ever had, rolled into human form. The president of The Knights of Hades, bikers, destroyers, death.

I've been here too long already and can see no light appearing to guide me to the exit. It was meant to be an in and out job. Go undercover at the MC club that is number one on the FBI to-do list. Men who stare at the law and raise their middle finger before causing devastation on a town that shivers in its shadow. Drugs, prostitution, money laundering, and contract killings. Nothing is too dark for the Knights of Hades, and I am the idiot the FBI sent in to gather information. Cut out their heart and leave them to bleed to death and I was a fool for ever thinking I was up to the job.

Tonight is my point of no return because tonight, I become his.

Taking some deep breaths of the rancid air that surrounds his soul, I plaster a blank look on my face and hope to hell the fear doesn't show in my eyes. Blaze is the man you never hoped to meet. Unlike the beast in the Disney story, this man has no redeeming features. He has no soul, no feeling, and no compassion.

I've watched him rule his club with a sword of terror and if he's pissed, the first person who upsets him meets their maker. He kills as if he's putting out the trash. No regard for human life, for feeling, for anything that makes the rest of us human. Now it's my turn.

"I'm sorry, Bonnie."

The whispered words of the woman next to me just increase my anxiety. She's sorry. One word that can't possibly excuse what's happening tonight.

My wedding.

I'm to become the latest casualty in a long line before me. Women who have captured the attention of the biggest bastard of them all. Taken as his old lady and used until the shine wears off. If they don't kill themselves, he does it for them and moves on to the next one. Like all sick predators, he uses time to his advantage and watches with the promise your end won't be pleasant.

He likes to play with his kill, stalk them, watch them try to think of every escape route possible. There is none. The only way out of this place is to burn in hell because that's where he sends you when he spies a new target.

My predecessor lasted two months. Not bad for a man who changes his partner more frequently than his underwear. There is nothing attractive about the man who wears the blood of his victims as war paint. I'm not sure how old he is, I'm guessing late forties. Dark hair turning a shade of gray, with a beard that disguises the many scars that come with the territory. He likes to cut, slice, and inflict the worse possible torture on his victims. Possibly because he has been the recipient of a knife more times than I can count. The scars on his face and body outline a dark soul and he is covered in them. Many have tried to slay the beast and ended up the one in the ground themselves. His scars are his battle cry and a knife his sword of choice. Now his focus is on me and my time's run out.

"What's takin' so long?"

He sounds irritable, which is not a good sign. Quickly, I turn and plaster a smile on my face.

"Coming right up."

I know better than to show any fear because he likes that the most and if I can brazen this out a little longer, I may escape a fate worse than death.

Sliding the beer across the bar, my heart sinks when he says ominously, "Deliver it personally."

My heart goes into freefall and thumps dangerously close to packing up on me completely. The noise in the bar stills as the rest of them watch a scene unfold they have seen a thousand times already and still find fascinating to watch.

Just the thought of that man's hands anywhere near me is enough to have me passing out in fright and disgust. I have never met a more unattractive man in my life, and it's not just because of his looks. His aftershave of choice is the bleeding souls of the damned that he cuts down without a thought for them or their families. He rapes, tortures, and ruins and I am next in line.

The anticipation in the air is thick as I grab the glass and move around the bar quickly, considering my options that appear to be in short supply right now. Maybe I can take him out with one smash of the glass and a quick slice to the jugular. They would probably thank me for it, but I know in my heart my body would soon fall onto his. These men have no regard for life at all and would relish the excuse to add another ghost to hell and not make it a pleasant transition to the afterlife.

Swallowing hard, I take every step as if it's my last and as I reach him, he knocks the beer out of my hand and I watch it fall to the ground, shattering on impact. The liquid spills on the scuffed wooden floor, and he growls, "On your knees."

The tears burn as I do as he says because to defy him would prolong my agony. It's best just to go along with it and look for the opportune moment to save myself from a fate worse than death - him.

I squeeze my eyes tightly shut and count down in my mind to the end of life as I know it. How has this happened? Reached the point that I was assured would never become a thing. My superiors told me they would have my back. Protect me and keep me safe in return for information. I've played my part; I've fed it back to them and now they have enough on the Knights to dress them in orange for life.

Where are they?

I hear them move behind me and know what happens next. I've seen it myself and know this is the night that will change my life forever. I am backed into a corner with no escape route and as I'm pulled to my feet, I stifle a scream and check the tears. I will not be broken.

"Strip her."

I know better than to resist, it will only make things worse, so as the clothes are sliced from my body with a couple of cuts from a blade, I try desperately hard not to think about the degrading scene that is unfolding right now.

I make no sound at all as I stand naked in the clubhouse providing a feast for a horny bunch of bikers and will myself not to react in any way that will prolong my mortification.

I feel his gaze ripping any pride from my soul as he openly stares and licks his lips, and as the soft fabric falls around my body, I feel the shiver pass through me as the sand reaches the bottom of the timer.

I know what I'm dressed in. A black wedding dress. Folds of fabric encase my body, decorated by the blood of the women who wore it before me.

Ripped, bloody and dripping in evil, this dress signifies the last shred of any decency I own. It chains me to him—the devil in the leather jacket that will soon be draped over my innocence.

Where are they?

I offer a last prayer to the gods who promised to protect me. Surely, they must have known this would happen. I told them more times than I can count. I was assured it was in hand. They had their information and were preparing to arrest the whole fucking club and every chapter associated with them. But when - it has to be now?

He stands.

"Bring in the priest."

CHAPTER 2

SNAKE

From my position I can see every breath she takes, every tear that forms and every thought in her head and I have never seen bravery like that wrapped up in desire. This woman is a goddess I never thought I'd see on earth. An unexpected treasure in a dark cave of madness.

The air is tense, the usual stench we breathe before going in for the kill. This is different. Different because she's there.

I shift, impatient to move this on, and the stark tones of my leader hold me back.

"Not yet." The barest whisper of a voice I would kill for. My best friend, the man I owe my life and my brother in every way but blood. Unless you count the liters we've spilled in the name of justice. The blood we wash off our hands and clothes as a daily ritual. As blood brothers go, we are more like twins and yet today I want to defy him so badly it physically hurts because I want to go in—now.

We watch the priest enter the room and I stifle a grin. For all the intensity surrounding me right now, Ryder's throaty chuckle brings a smile to my lips.

"Fucking suits him, the bastard."

We watch our brother make the short walk to the unhappy bride and from the look on the face of her groom the honeymoon happens as soon as he says 'I do.' He is staring at her in a haze of lust driven by depravation. We've been told he allows one sentence of ownership that in his eyes makes them wed before God, before he rips his bride's soul from inside her before the priest even leaves. Bastard. Dirty fucking bastard and my fist clenches around the knife I hold in my hand, ready to inflict his final scar. The one that will end his miserable life and make the world a better place.

"Easy tiger."

Ryder's voice shatters the silence and I wonder how he does this. Knows what I'm thinking before the thought even enters my head.

I say nothing because words are the last thing on my mind right now. Its action needed now because that frightened woman is doing something strange to my heart. Reminding me I have one.

We watch Brewer head into the pack and Ryder stills beside me. We have our rifles trained on the president and his second in command, Bones Halligan. A man who has acted as judge, jury and executioner in many poor men's lives and I know that one sniff of something going down would end that girl's life in a heartbeat. The rest of our men are trained on every fucking member in that clubhouse, and we have set up a ring of steel around the perimeter.

Brought in to finish a job the way only we can and sweep the garbage from the streets, enabling decent Americans to sleep safely at night. No repercussions and no questions asked. I love my job.

Brewer advances dressed like a girl in a long white robe hiding his killer's instinct. The real priest is safe in the church praying for our souls because we discovered the stupid fucking pricks didn't even check him out.

Big mistake.

Now we have one of our own entering the lion's den, and his life is the most important one in there.

And the girl.

There's a strange feeling of protectiveness that is blurring my usual sharp lines. Setting me on edge and taking my mind away from the job. Bonnie Anderson. Undercover Fed and sacrificial lamb to the slaughter. It makes my blood heat knowing those bastards sent her here to a certain death. Mind you, death would be the kinder option because it's what happens before that will burn her soul, leaving her in ashes as she steps out of her devastated body to leave this life behind. Yes, there is only one outcome for the brave, misguided Fed - death by bastard. Well, it takes an even bigger one to overturn the decision, and that is not happening today, or any day I'm watching over her.

Blaze looks up as Brewer enters and checks him out. Two of his men move beside him and pat him down for concealed weapons. Luckily, the only weapon that man needs is his fists and was the perfect trojan horse to send into the battle. Brewer is third in command of the Twisted Reapers MC. I am second and Ryder King is first. Our president and the biggest bastard that walks this earth. Ex-Navy SEAL and badassed military assassin, heading up our particular branch of rough justice. We are all cut from the same cloth, shaped from the same mold, and live a life many would never even dream about.

Paid government assassins detailed with sweeping the trash from the streets and hiding the evidence so no questions are asked.

We're good at our job, which is a good thing for that little lady who has my interest.

"He's clean."

The rough tones of one of the bikers tell his president what he needs to know and I watch with interest the desperation in the Fed's eyes. She's folding, crumbling under pressure and may resort to doing something stupid.

Once again, I shift impatiently because if she dies on my watch, I'm liable to freak the fuck out and murder the bastards bare handed.

"Wait!"

Ryder's tone is terse and commanding and I fucking hate him right now, but I settle down and wait, the promise growing in my eyes as I direct them toward the bastard who is about to meet his maker.

"Get on with it."

Blaze is rude and straight to the point, and Brewer just nods and stands before the unhappy couple.

Blaze grabs Bonnie's arm and pulls her roughly beside him and I feel fury heat my blood as he grabs her ass hard and she yelps a little.

He growls ominously, "I said get on with it."

Brewer nods and to anyone watching he looks pleasant, amenable and as if he hasn't got a fucking clue. It almost makes me laugh as he says the words the bastard wants to hear.

"Do you, Blaze, take Bonnie to be your lawfully wedded wife in the eyes of God and your family?"

"I do."

Blaze leers at Bonnie and she looks as if she's about to hurl in his face. Praying to see that happen, I'm denied as Brewer says, "And Bonnie, do you take Blaze as your lawfully wedded…"

"She does."

Brewer raises his eyes as Bonnie shakes her head, imploring him with her eyes to rescue her from the worst situation she has probably ever been in.

"Then I now pronounce you…"

As Brewer prepares to utter the trigger word, time stands still.

CHAPTER 3

BONNIE

I can't do this. My heart is racing faster than I think it ever has, even after basic training when we ran 20 kilometers in the mountains with full kit. I'm not cut out for this shit. I should be investigating murders, kidnappings, drugs, anything but going undercover as an informant for the bastards I work for. When I signed up, it wasn't for this. To be a fuck toy for a bastard who will probably kill me in the end. Did I say probably, I should have said definitely because my life is flashing before my eyes right now and it's because this is really happening?

I'm marrying the devil in hell and there is absolutely nothing I can do about it.

I'm not sure why, but the priest doesn't even look the type. Knowing Blaze, he is probably one of his men anyway, and this is all for show. Maybe our information was wrong, that he is deeply religious and uses his prayer beads as a defense against his sins. Commits the crime and then demands forgiveness—or else.

Religious my ass because no man with a pure soul would

ever live like he does and shows me what madness lies inside his brain. He is damaged beyond repair, and this charade is nothing but that. A crazy show to make him feel better about doing something so wrong he should be locked up for life and sentenced to the electric chair at the end of it.

I hear him speak and when he pulls me roughly beside him and grabs my ass, I can't help the desperate yelp finding an outlet. I hate my weakness. I'm a fighter, not a victim and as the 'service' begins, I gather my training around me. No, today is not the day Bonnie Anderson folds under pressure, because if I have to die, I would rather go out fighting.

As soon as the priest opens his mouth to say the final words that cement my fate, I reach down and grab the shard of glass that I folded in my dress that the bastards never saw happening.

Right. Before. Their. Eyes.

As the priest opens his mouth, I grip the glass so hard I feel my blood coat it and with one hard shove, stick it straight through the bastard's neck. The look in his eyes will live with me forever as he stares in disbelief as the blood gushes from the severed artery, spilling his life onto the black, blood-soaked dress that doubles as a funeral shroud.

He makes a strange gurgling sound and then the shit really hits the fan.

The priest lurches forward and pushes me to the ground, covering me with his body as several shots ring out. Shouting and bullets ripping through the clubhouse end many lives as they scream all around me in hurt and anger. I feel pain and wonder if I've been hit and a low whisper sounds above the noise, "Stay down."

The priest is heavy on my back and I wonder if he's been hit. I can't move an inch out of fear of losing my life and am grateful for the protection he gives me.

The air is full of death and stinks of justice as one by one the Knights of Hades fall around me.

They're here, the FBI has attacked and I silently offer my thanks to God for saving me. The relief is like nothing I've ever felt before as the tears slowly trickle down my face, spilling onto the dusty floor where Blaze's blood runs like a river to Hell.

Five minutes maybe, ten at most, I lie cowering under a human shield, praying he is alive at least. As the smoke clears and the noise stills to silence, it's replaced by a different form of energy. Groans of pain are swiftly silenced by the bullet from a gun and only when the final groan is sent on its way, does the body shift from my back and I hear a terse, "That was close."

I daren't look because these voices don't sound like the usual ones I hear, they are rough, crude and laced with danger and instinctively I know this isn't over yet.

Strong hands pull me up and before I can even see who they belong to, I am hauled over a hard shoulder and carried from the room.

I'm not sure what to do, struggle perhaps because this isn't usual protocol. Then again, what is? I've never been in a gunfight before and I'm struggling to keep up.

The cool air hits my skin as we head outside and I make to struggle before a terse angry voice growls, "So help me, I'll spank this fine ass of yours if you try to get away. What the fuck were you thinking?"

His voice shocks me into silence and I stop moving, even breathing in fear of his promise because if this guy's a Fed, I'm Sleeping fucking Beauty.

To my surprise, I am deposited sharply on a bike and a leather jacket is wrapped around my shivering shoulders and a helmet rammed firmly down on my head. Before I can get a look at my rescuer, captor, I'm not sure what the fuck he is, he shifts before me and starts the engine that sounds as angry as he is.

Pulling my arms tight around his waist, I'm tempted to run, escape somehow, but he gives me no chance because he's off at speed, leaving me clinging on for grim death.

He rides fast. Furious and with a confidence that tells me I'm not going to die on this journey at least. Maybe he has a more painful ending in store and I tremble not just from the cold but from the fear running like ice through my veins.

I suppose I'm a little in shock. I just killed a man. Technically he's a monster, but the law would take some convincing on that.

I killed a man.

I have to repeat the words in my mind because that was the first thing I thought to do. Fight before flight and I only had a split second to save myself from a certain painful, excruciating death. He wasn't going to keep me long. I know how he works. I heard enough hushed conversations regarding my predecessors to know he has a short attention span. Usually after the wedding he rapes his bride before his club. Then he drags her upstairs and chains her to his bed before raping her on repeat and breaking her spirit. Sometimes he let his men have a turn, depending on how generous he was feeling. Yes, I heard the whispers, the tales of a dismal ending that was in my immediate future.

The tears blind me as I think on what I could be doing right now, and if I had my time again, I wouldn't change a thing. Blaze was a monster of the worst kind, and I did women everywhere a favor in reducing him to dust.

Now I'm in a different kind of danger because since when did the FBI wear leather and ride Harleys? No, from the writing on the back of the leather jacket staring me in the face, I've just met the Grim Reaper. Twisted Reaper MC are the words, and I'm in no doubt it's exactly what it says on the tin.

This man is another biker and apparently, I have just been caught up in a biker war. No, I'm not safe yet, so I must keep my wits about me and take the first opportunity that presents itself to escape and that will start as soon as this machine reaches its destination.

CHAPTER 4

SNAKE

I am so angry I can taste it. The bitter stench of missed opportunities and one very exciting one is conflicting my mood. I wanted to end Blaze's life so badly I feel as if I've been denied my moment of satisfaction. Then again, now I have an interesting prisoner to deal with because the instructions were to take the girl and hide her. Ryder directed his words to Tyson, but I spoke up, causing him to raise his eyes and smirk. I couldn't help it because I am the only man for this job because the thought of her on the back of anyone else's bike sends a surprising surge of jealously straight to my heart.

Ryder just shrugged and carried on issuing his orders, leaving me with an interesting prospect lined up.

The minute she ended Blaze's life; all hell broke out. Brewer launched himself on her as we fired, taking out the Knights in a blaze of gunfire - the irony of which was not lost on me.

Bonnie dealt with the president herself and part of me admires her for that. Then again, it could have cost her life and I will *never* be ok with that.

Now I'm to take her to the cabin and keep her prisoner

until Ryder finishes the job, and that's more than ok with me. To be honest, I was a little surprised when he agreed. He usually likes to keep me closer to home, I'm always by his side and this could take some time. Maybe he saw the glint in my eye and heard the purpose in my voice. Bonnie is mine and now they all know not to touch.

I've never been keen to settle on one woman before. Hell, we have quite a candy store back at the compound to choose from. But Bonnie, there is something about her that rattles my soul. She's different, and I can't put my finger on why.

Now she's clinging on tight and I'm loving every second and I'm almost tempted to take the long way round just to prolong this pleasure.

The only thing stopping me is the blood on her hands and I know not all of it is his. I saw the cut from the shard of glass and the terror in her eyes. She's not ok. She may think she is, but I'm guessing she will be dealing with some serious shit in the coming days and will need watching.

So, reluctantly, I head up the track to the cabin we have nearby, one of many bolt holes littered around the country. Nobody would come here unless they have a death wish, and most probably don't know of its existence.

I come to a stop outside the cabin and feel a strange sense of anticipation building. There's something about the wind of change. It blows up when you least expect it, and I'm feeling it whipping around me now as I reach for the key in my pocket.

One moment's distraction is all she needs because suddenly, she launches herself from the bike and starts running.

Cursing, I give chase as she heads off through the trees and the darkness swallows her up like a welcome safety blanket.

Stopping, I listen and hear a twig crack and I think hard. Trying to second guess her route, I head off in pursuit softly and keeping an ear to the ground to listen out for any signs of her position.

The blanket of darkness disguises the rage in my heart because I am so pissed at this foolish act of desperation. What is she thinking? Dressed like the bride of Frankenstein and leaking blood is sure to bring the wild animals out from the shadows, eyeing up their next meal. It's just a good thing I am no different, and the thought of anything other than me getting their hands on this woman is just not happening.

Only my heart provides a steady rhythm as I set off in pursuit, and as I move through the trees, I call on my training mixed with instinct to guide me to her.

She's good though, I'll give her that at least because it takes all my ability even to know where she's heading.

I'm a silent predator and she's a clever girl because to anyone else the only sound in the forest is that of nature. We are both moving in silence, not an easy thing to do in darkness, and yet the sliver of light from the moon is a welcome torch.

Every so often I stop and check for tracks or signs of recent disturbance, telling me what I need to know and it's only when the track runs cold, I know I'm close and stand for a minute to get my bearings.

I notice several large trees and imagine her to be hiding behind one of them, hoping I'll pass so she can double back to the bike. It's what I would do, and I wonder if she's there already and has achieved something no one has before. Outwitted the snake.

A slight rustle in the trees alerts me to something above me and I smile to myself. Gotcha.

Pretending to leave, I start off and as soon as I'm out of sight I double back.

Making sure to keep a wide angle, I head back toward the cabin and wait.

Sure enough, it takes only ten minutes before I see a slight shape dressed like a vampire heading out of the shadows, looking behind her anxiously. As she steps nearer the bike, I move behind her and with one flick of my wrist, spin her to the ground and relish the scream that tears from her lips.

However, that's the only thing that indicates her fear because suddenly I'm faced with a worthy opponent.

She catches me off-guard with a quick knee in the groin, and my grunt of pain is the only indication it met its mark.

Keeping my hand firmly wrapped around her wrist, I growl, "For fuck's sake, stop fighting me, I'm helping you."

"Asshole." Her gritted words make me smile, which soon fades as she twists her wrist free and punches me straight in the eye. She doesn't stop there and brings her leg up and around, taking my ankles from under me, and as I fall forward, she rolls to the side and elbows me sharply in the ribs. Fuck me, this is harder than I thought and as she takes off, I see her grab a small rock lying beside her and I grin. I knew there was something about this woman, it's almost a shame to end this.

She heads toward my bike, and I wonder if she believes she stands any chance of getting away. Perhaps she thinks I left the keys in my haste to catch up with her.

I hear her curse as she reaches it and as I give chase, she yells, "You come anywhere near me and I'll kill you. I'm trained and know what I'm doing, so you've been warned."

Biting back a smile, I slow my pace and put my hands in the air.

"You win."

As I approach, I see the disheveled woman staring at me with suspicion and my heart does something strange. It leaps into life as I see a woman looking so scared and vulnerable, fighting to make herself appear unconcerned and in control. I already know she is the most attractive woman I have ever met, and my cock stirs as it registers its interest.

However, I may be interested in her, but she is most definitely not returning the favor as she hisses, "Give me the keys."

"Sure, I'll be glad to be rid of you."

She looks taken aback and as I reach for the keys, I see her hitch her breath and stare as if in shock.

Holding them high in the air, I growl, "Come and get them."

"Do you think I'm an idiot?"

She sounds angry and I see her eyes flash in the darkness as she runs on adrenalin.

"No, I think you're tired, frightened and out of your depth. I think you're hurting because you just killed a man, and he left his mark on the wound on your hand. I think you're struggling to make sense of anything right now and think tearing off on my bike to safety will guarantee yours. It won't.

"Says you, the man who kidnapped me and murdered a room full of people in the name of a twisted war. I know what just happened."

"Then tell me, this I've got to hear."

"It's obvious - a biker war. You took out the competition, am I right?"

"Not even close."

I dangle the keys before her and say softly, "So, you want your freedom, how are you gonna earn it?"

"I'm not. I owe you nothing."

She holds her head at an angle that shows she's not compromising and I like that—a lot.

"So, Bonnie."

She steps back a little. "You know my name."

"Yes, darlin', I know your name. I know who you are, why you were there, and what was about to happen next. I know you were desperate, probably wondering why your unit hadn't saved you by now, and I'm guessing that's why you took matters into your own hands. You see, Bonnie, I know this because I am the unit they sent, although a little earlier than planned."

"What's that supposed to mean?"

Her voice shakes as she struggles to understand my meaning, and I shrug. "There was no one coming for you tonight, darlin'. They were hoping your fate would be sealed long before they stormed that building and it appears that the only one who didn't know was you."

CHAPTER 5

BONNIE

My head hurts, my whole body hurts, and now my soul hurts. They weren't coming. Who is this man?

Feeling a little blinded by circumstance, I shake my head. "You're lying."

"Why would I?"

The beast watching me is like nothing I've ever seen before. Unlike the Knights of Hades, he has a gentle air about him. More refined and seems kinder somehow. Then again, physically he's Lucifer himself. Closely cropped hair that gives him a dark edge and dark eyes that could tear a person's soul from inside them with just one look. He is possibly the most muscled man I have ever met given the width of his arms and the snake that decorates one of them inching up to his neck, makes me shiver inside.

This man is a beast in every way and I must remind myself of that as I falter slightly, "If you know who I am then remind me, I'd love to know."

His low chuckle seems at odds with the situation as he says

in a husky voice, "Bonnie Anderson, undercover Fed. Sent in to gather intel on the Knights of Hades for your superior, Jefferson Atkins."

I swallow—hard.

He continues.

"You've been feeding back intelligence for three weeks already and was running out of time. We stormed the building just before that ran out because you were about to be brutally murdered in front of the whole fucking club."

His words cause a huge shock to hit my body like an earthquake and I whisper, "Murdered."

He says almost kindly, "Our own intelligence gave us the facts, and we went in to save you, Bonnie. To remove you from the situation and keep you safe. It's why we're here in the middle of nowhere, removing you from life until we work out the rest. Color in the picture and reveal the madness you've got yourself caught in. So, word of advice, darlin', trust the beast this time because I've only got your best interests at heart."

My tears have frozen behind my eyes in a moment of indecision. Is this true - it can't be? He's obviously lying, but why?

He says kindly, "Think on it for the night. I mean you no harm and if anything, I'm in need of sleep and food and not necessarily in that order. Let me sort your hand out and allow you to clean up. I give you my word I'm not here to harm you."

He makes it seem so easy, normal even, but he could be lulling me into a false sense of security. Classic tactics to bring doubt into the situation. Then again, I need to know more because if my superior was never coming for me, I want to know why?

Recognizing I don't have much choice, I nod and say tersely, "Ok, on one condition."

"Name it."

"You stay the fuck away from me."

His next words cause me to shiver inside as he growls, "You may want to reconsider that request because, darlin', sometimes the stars align and fate plays a blinder and this is one of those times. I am your best friend, your only hope of surviving this shit storm, and you are gonna learn to trust me if it kills me. So, drop the attitude, pack away those principles and settle in because I hate to break it to you but honey, we're home."

He jerks his head toward the cabin nestling in the shadows and says wearily, "Come, there's a bed in there with your name on it and I'm guessing you would be grateful to ditch the bride of Frankenstein look."

Looking down at the blood-soaked dress that has dressed the souls of the damned before me, I nod in defeat.

"Ok, have it your way but one false move and I'll end you, just like I did Blaze."

I stare at him defiantly and to my surprise he laughs softly, "Interesting, death by Bonnie, what a way to go."

He appears to find his words funny and just heads toward the cabin, and I see him turn a key in the lock and flick on a light, the beam lighting up the ground before it. As he stands framed in the doorway, his huge body cuts out the light as he says quickly, "Come on, I'll fix us a couple of drinks and take a look at your hand. You have my word you're safe."

Safe. Am I, really? Something about this man tells me I'm anything but safe, but not for the usual reasons. He's dark, mysterious, and wears his honor like a battle cry. It surrounds him. There's something about him that makes me feel safe, comfortable even, and yet am I? I'm not sure about that so I step hesitantly toward him wondering if a bad night is about to get a lot worse.

∼

My first look at the cabin surprises me. From the outside it appears a ruin, a ramshackle pile of wood with no redeeming features. But this place is modern, homey even, and I blink in surprise as he heads toward a log burner and sets about lighting a fire.

"There's a bathroom through there if you want to clean up."

He nods toward a door at the side and adds, "You'll find a closet of clothes, choose something that fits if you can. Sorry about the choice but we're not used to entertaining and any woman that usually comes here doesn't need clothes, anyway."

"That's disgusting." My voice holds a sharp edge, making him laugh. "I'm no gentleman, Bonnie, you'll find that out soon enough."

"No, I won't because you promised to stay away. If you back down on that, I will have to kill you."

My words are edged in defiance and colored in by threats, but he obviously doesn't see that because he throws his head back and laughs. "Good answer, darlin', now, conversation over. You have your wish, your privacy, and you can clean up safe in the knowledge I'm staying right here until you return."

Something tells me I can trust him on that, so I spin on my heel and create some distance between us. I need that more than anything right now because despite how ferocious this man is, my body is drawn to him in a sort of primal urge. Feeling disgusted with myself, I wrestle open the door and step inside a little piece of heaven.

My eyes are wide as I take in a modern bedroom. Basic but clean and tasteful and I blink as I see another door, slightly open, revealing a large bathroom with a walk-in shower.

Wandering around the room in surprise, I take in the clean sheets and fluffy folded towels. The air smells fresh and nothing about how I imagined a place like this to look.

As I catch sight of my reflection in the mirror, I could cry because I look scared shitless. Wandering over, I look at an image of a ruined soul. My blood red hair is interlaced with twigs and leaves and could do with a good brush. My face is whiter than snow and my eyes look dark and troubled. Dirt replaces make-up and there's a haunted expression looking back at me.

Just seeing the dress makes me rip it off in disgust because if I'm doing anything with this, it's burning it on that fire outside.

Quickly, I turn on the shower and stand under its cleansing cascade, intent on washing away the bad memory of my almost death.

I know this guy was right about that, at least. I saw the madness in Blaze's eyes and knew he had more than marriage on his mind. If what he says is true, I was about to meet an extremely violent end and I shiver inside.

The blood from my wound runs like a river down the drain, and I shiver uncontrollably. Kill or be killed. It was a moment of survival instinct that led me to commit a crime I could be incarcerated for. Those disbelieving eyes that stared at me with surprise more than anything else, before his final gasp of air told him the game was over - for him, anyway.

I'm still in it because I'm in no doubt this is all a game to that beast outside. His look of amusement and the fear in my eyes makes me angry and yet, there's something I can't shake about him. The feeling that he's important to me somehow. Maybe he's my ticket to safety. It doesn't feel like that, but why bring me here? Is he right, was I going to end my career tonight along with my life?

If I need anything right now, it's answers and I'm guessing the man through that door knows way more than he's letting on, so with a sigh, I turn off the jets and step outside, shivering in the sudden cool breeze that accompanies the diminishing steam from the hot jets of water that cleared my mind as well as my body.

Now it's all about survival—mine and it's up to me to get to the root of the problem and deal with it appropriately.

Survival is the most important thing right now, and I must keep my wits about me and guard my heart because something tells me it's in more danger than it's ever been in before.

CHAPTER 6

SNAKE

I knew this was a good idea. Every word from her lips makes me smile and I could watch her all day. She's so scared yet trying hard to gather her bravery around her and use it against me. It won't work—it never does because there is not a person alive who intimidates me, although that could be about to change because I think she may be the exception to that particular rule.

Once I get the fire going, I set about making coffee and rustling up something to eat. It's been a long day and the weeks ahead will be challenging because my orders are to keep her here. I wasn't lying when I said she needed removing from life because there is something festering at the heart of justice and we need to find the cancer and cut it out.

By the time the coffee has brewed, she returns and I hide the grin that threatens to annoy her even further when I see her dressed in combats and a t-shirt. They are at least four sizes too big, and she has tied them at the waist with a belt that looks as if it spans that small waist at least four times. The look of disgust on her face does make me smile, and she snaps, "Do you find something amusing?"

"Is that the best you could find?"

She tosses back her wet hair and says angrily, "I don't know who does your shopping around here but I'm guessing it's a whore because those clothes are disgusting and if you think I'm about to dress like one for your own sick, perverted pleasure, then you're wrong?"

Thinking on who chose them, she's not far off and I laugh. "10/10 for observation."

"You mean…"

"Yes, darlin', a whore did choose your clothes and probably thought that whoever ended up on babysitting duty could use a bit of eye candy."

"Well, I'm not here for your pleasure, I'm here because you kidnapped me and what I want to know, is why you can't just take me home?"

Her face mirrors her fear and disgust, and the fact she's dressed in clothes far too big for her gives her a vulnerability that is way more powerful than the sexy clothes Kitty must have packed.

Sighing, I point to the couch. "Take a seat and I'll explain, but not before you drink this."

Handing her a mug of coffee, I note the reluctant gratitude in her eyes as she says tersely, "Ok, have it your way but just for the record, I am really not happy about this."

She grudgingly takes the coffee and sits on the couch, wrapping her legs under her, and I see the weariness in her expression as she accepts her fate—for now.

Taking the seat opposite, I relish the crackle of flames and bask in the heat as I say evenly, "The Knights of Hades have been under observation for some time."

She rolls her eyes. "You don't say, Sherlock, why do you think I was there, for the hell of it?"

Resisting the urge to throw her over my knee and spank that fine ass, I bite back my irritation and put it down to fear and say gruffly, "Yes you were there to feed back intel, and you did your job well under extremely trying circumstances."

"You don't say." Once again, she rolls her eyes and my palm itches as I finally snap.

Fixing her with my best 'shut the fuck up' look, she appears to retreat as she sinks back against the couch. "Now, listen good, darlin' because the attitude has got to go. If you think this is what I want to be doing with my time, you're wrong. Have some fucking gratitude because we just saved your life back there and I am *not* the bad guy here. If you want to leave, then be my guest and save me from babysitting a petulant child. Now, shut the fuck up and listen, or so help me god, I'll bend you over my knee and spank that fine ass until you learn some manners."

Her gasp of horror makes me almost consider cutting out the words and taking action because I am done with this soft shit. I have tried so hard to be understanding but her attitude is rubbing me up the wrong way and if she thought the Knights were bastards, she hasn't met the biggest one of all.

Thinking it best to remove myself from a very tempting situation, I stand and the fear in her eyes as she looks at me irritates the hell out of me and I snap, "I'm going out before I do something we'll both regret."

I don't even wait for an answer and slam the cabin door behind me on the way out, creating a physical barrier between us because god help us all, I'm so close to revealing that I'm worse than every fucking Knight of Hades rolled into one.

The darkness wraps me in protection as I head to my bike and sit astride it, reaching for a smoke, which irritates the shit out of me because I'm trying to kick the habit. Not on this mission, that's becoming way too obvious because this woman is testing my patience and I'm in danger of failing. Briefly, I wonder if this was such a good idea. I should have let Tyson take this one after all. The trouble is, I felt something when I saw her. She's so different from the usual girls I meet. A defiant bundle of every wet dream I ever had, and her attitude is one of the reasons I'm so attracted to her. I like a woman who gives back as good as she gets, and not many have that ability around me. I know I'm intimidating, a beast to many, but I hide a heart inside that's been empty for far too long.

Living the life I do—we all do, tears down any humanity and drapes you in sin. I'm a killer and there's no dressing up that fact. We just re-enacted a scene from Kill Bill back there and didn't even take a second look. It's a normal day at the office that usually ends inside one of the whores who lives back at the compound. We lose ourselves in femininity to bring us back from the edge of hell and yet here I am, stuck with a sassy attitude wrapped up in every wet dream I ever had. The fact she obviously hates me is inconvenient, and I'm not a patient man who can deal with waiting while she figures shit out.

My cell vibrating interrupts my dark thoughts and I say gruffly, "What's up?"

"Just checkin' in, what have you discovered?"

"That I should never have let you fucking talk me into this."

The low chuckle on the other end of the line irritates me and he growls, *"Be careful what you wish for."*

"So," I exhale sharply, "How long can I expect to babysit a brat?"

"Who knows? For all the FBI know, their operative is still alive and kicking and safely, or should I say, still in danger at the gates of hell."

"What's the plan?"

"Brewer's gathering intel but it could take a few more days. We need to plan this carefully because the man in charge wants discretion on this because any sign of trouble at the heart of democracy will not paint him in a good light."

"Fine, but you tell Brewer to get his ass in gear because I'm liable to snap at any moment and you better not give me any of that character shit you usually spout because it's not going to work on me."

"Easy soldier, you forget you chose this mission and as you know, some are harder than others."

"Fuck you, Ryder, call me when you have news."

I cut the call and feel the irritation rattle my cage. Lighting my smoke, I sit on the bike and try to calm the fuck down because one more sassy word out of those lips may make me do something I will most definitely regret.

CHAPTER 7

BONNIE

Thank god he's gone. The moment that door slammed, I felt the relief hit me hard. Now I'm alone, the thoughts I'm trying to deal with crowd around me as I try to make sense of what's happening.

I just killed a man.

I can't shake that and shiver as I think of an image that will live with me forever. Those disbelieving eyes, the startled gasp and the sound of death as he struggled to take his last breath. The blood that spurted from his severed artery and saturated my humanity is something I can never change and now I'm labeled a killer, a cold-blooded murderer because that was what it was. I knew what I had to do, but it doesn't make it any easier to live with. I keep on telling myself he deserved to die. Thinking of all the women he murdered in the past, probably wearing that black dress, makes me shiver and the prickle of fear and disgust consumes my body.

The blaze has been extinguished, but at what price? I can't deal with it and toss back the coffee and look around me for something stronger to dull my senses. I need to deal with this, but I can't. There is no counseling here in the forest, just an angry beast who scares the hell out of me.

Quickly, I check the cupboards for any sign of alcohol that will numb my senses. Help me sleep because I doubt I'll do it naturally. My search reveals one good thing at least—there are two bedrooms on either side of this living room, so at least I won't have the problem of the sleeping arrangements to deal with because that beast's bag is resting on another huge bed and I'm grateful for that.

I'm almost tempted to search his bag for evidence, or at least something to help me take the edge off this madness. However, there's still the part of me that abides by the rules holding me back. Rifling through another person's things doesn't sit well with me, despite the fact I'm a cop and used to searching for information.

Heading back to the fire, I think about my job. I'm a proud cop, I always was. Doing well at training and earning a place in the department I always wanted to join. The FBI. Maybe it's because of my father. He was a good cop. Always proud to wear the uniform and defend the freedom of the country. He tried so hard and was rewarded by joining the very department I served under. He never made the grade and his stay there was short, which is why I studied hard, plotted my path to success and clawed my way into a department only a few get to wear the badge. Well, I wear mine with pride, which is why I was happy to go undercover because the Knights of Hades were the worst kind of problem. Organized crime at its most basic and what I saw within those walls will haunt me forever.

Now I'm one of them. A killer, a person who lost touch with what's right. If I had just held back for one more second, they would have come in anyway. I had time, not much but some at least, and now I have a memory to live with that could drag me under.

I slump on the couch and feel the frustration tearing me up

inside. I need to forget, to dull my senses, anything but sit here thinking of something that I can't deal with right now. All I have is a surly companion who I am glad to see the back of. Just the thought of what that man is capable of scares the shit out of me, and now I need my training more than ever. To defend myself from him.

It's obvious he's interested. Just the way he looks at me tells me that. Then again, they all looked at me like that. The Knights wanted me, but I fought them off and I was given a pass because I was a marked woman. Once again, I shiver as I remember whose woman I was to be.

His. Blaze. The President. Bastard.

Sighing, I curl up on the couch and contemplate trying to sleep. However, I know the nightmares are jostling for position to bring me down. I can't sleep, I'm too wired for that and maybe that beast is the distraction I need. Prod him a little to distract my mind from the horror it must now live with. Maybe he will finish the job and put me out of my misery because I'm not sure I can live with what I've done.

Decision made, I edge off the couch and head toward the door. Then, taking a deep breath, I open it and blink as my eyes adjust to the darkness.

All I can see is the tip of a cigarette from the direction of his bike and I head toward it like a misguided moth about to be cut down for being so foolish.

"Have you got a spare?"

My voice is soft, rough around the edges and laced with regret, and he growls, "No."

"That's a bit rude, isn't it?"

"Yes."

Shifting on my feet, I wrap my arms around my chest and shiver a little more from the results of my actions than the cold.

"Do you have any alcohol, beer maybe, whiskey would do?"

"No."

He exhales sharply and says in a husky voice. "If you're looking for comfort in the bottle, you won't find it here."

"Why not?"

"Because there isn't any, obviously."

His sarcastic drawl irritates me and I snap. "Then go and get some, dumbass."

Have you ever wished you could catch the words that fall from your lips and snatch them back before they hit, because I feel that now as he tosses the cigarette to the ground and stamps on it sharply?

I see his eyes flash in the darkness as he says angrily, "What did you just say?"

Trying to brazen it out, I snap back, "You heard me."

In one swift move, he reaches out and grabs my wrist and pulls me across his bike, where he's sitting. Before I can even react, he pulls down my pants and delivers one swift, sharp blow to my ass and the force of it causes me to cry out in pain and horror. Before I can even fight back, another one lands and I scream into the black hole of hell. I think he hits me five times before pulling my pants up and shoving me off the bike, where I fall to a heap on the ground staring at him in humiliated anger.

He just stares at me through those dead eyes and I try really hard but no words come out and I just feel the tears building behind my eyes.

Suddenly, it hits me hard, what happened before, the position I'm in, the humiliation of what just happened and from nowhere it comes. The pain finds an outlet and I well and truly lose my shit.

The tears run like rapids down my face as I hug my knees and lower my head, sobbing as if I'm two years old. It's certainly how I feel after the worst humiliation a woman can suffer.

I don't care that he's watching, I don't care that he does nothing, just silently sits back and enjoys the show. But I need this. I need to let it all out because I'm struggling to breathe because of what I've done.

I'm not sure for how long I sob in the dirt at the feet of a beast, and I don't even register when strong arms lift me into an even stronger chest. Those same arms cradle my head and pull me close, and just feeling the comfort they bring makes me grateful for that at least. He carries me inside and kicks the door shut and then sits on the couch, holding me like a baby. Once again, this is humiliation at its finest, but I don't care anymore. I need something, someone to take away the bitter taste of criminality. Something to chase away the shadows and bring me back to the light. I have started a fatal path tonight and I know that, so maybe that's why I can't deal with what happened, knowing that I will never be the same again. I fell so hard into oblivion and there was nothing to break my fall, so being comforted by a demon is the best I can expect.

CHAPTER 8

SNAKE

I hate myself. I lost it and I'm not proud of what I've done. Why are women so hard to deal with? If a man spoke to me like that, I wouldn't hesitate to punch his lights out. Nobody speaks to me like I'm a piece of shit, and I forgot who I was dealing with for a moment. If I'm angry at anything it's that, and as she folded at my feet, I felt like the biggest bastard that ever lived.

Now I've destroyed her. Just seeing her crying in the dirt made me feel like breaking something. I don't hurt women, hell, the last thing I want is to go down that road, so I scooped her up and brought her inside. Knowing this is more for me than for her, I need to make amends, make good on my actions and as I cradle her, my arms tighten just a little more than usual. Leaning down, I am tempted to bury my face in her hair and take comfort in the scent of an angel to forgive me for what I just did.

Instead, I rock her gently and feel like an even bigger bastard when I realize it's because I'm enjoying it and not because it's purely for her benefit.

After a while, the sobs subside a little and she leans closer and her steady breathing tells me she's drifted off into some kind of sleep. I know how she's feeling, hell my first kill still lives with me today. I don't think anything prepares you for that—ever and I know she will struggle to come to terms with what she's done.

The fire crackles in the grate and I find my own eyes closing. It's been a helluva day and sleep is what's needed now. Tomorrow we can work out the details but for now I just need my bed but I'm strangely reluctant to let go of this woman who has snuggled into my chest, making me feel strangely protective over her.

Images of her naked body fill my mind as I remember what an angel looks like in hell. The thought of what she was about to face makes me delirious with rage, but she's safe now. Despite the fact I want her so badly, I'm a man who can control his most basic instincts. The priority now is saving Bonnie because the fact remains, she may have had a temporary reprieve but somebody wants her dead and I wonder how she will deal with that.

Sometime in the early hours, I carry her to bed. As I lower her onto it, her hair fans out either side of her beautiful face and in sleep she looks at peace. Her lips have settled into a soft comfort and I imagine myself tasting the candy within. Her lashes are long and dark against her white alabaster skin and the smudges on her face are where the tears have dried along with her mascara. Her breathing is even telling me she's in a happier place right now and as she moans in her sleep, I imagine what it would feel like to lie beside such a woman.

Strangely, I dip my head and kiss her softly on the cheek. I'm not sure why, it just feels right to do so. She shivers a little and a smile ghosts her lips, making me feel a little better about myself.

I'm not used to seeing a woman like her. I live with whores who have no emotion in their eyes when they look at me. They want me but I'm not the only one and I wonder what true love feels like. To know you are with the one person who loves you, every tainted part of your soul, and accepts you, anyway. They don't want what you can give them physically but is as possessive as hell over the emotional part of you. I fuck many women, and that's all it is. A fuck to drive away the images of a bloody day at the office. Now, watching an angel sleep, someone innocent who doesn't live this life by choice but by duty, to do something good, I am torn. I want her, but I want better for her. I want her to find peace and live her best life.

This woman deserves the best of everything, and I am the opposite of that. I have no right to even think I'm on her level, and so reluctantly I turn away and leave her behind. Heading instead to my usual bed for one, I lie back and imagine what it's like to share more than just sex with someone. Someone like her—her.

∽

I'M up early and my first thought is for the woman in the next room. Strangely, I feel anxious. What if she woke and left already? She could have. I let sleep claim my usual alertness and as I drag on my clothes, I head off in search of her.

Thinking better of knocking in case she's still sleeping, I inch the door open and look inside.

My heart leaps with relief when I see her tangled hair dangling from the bed as she lies with her arm hanging toward the floor. She's out cold and that's the best thing for her. So, smiling to myself, I head back outside and set about gathering wood for the fire.

Once my usual chores are done, I step into the shower and rinse off the weariness of the previous day. By the time I'm dressed and decent, I head outside and notice the sun is already high in the sky. It's gonna be a good day, I can feel it. The birds are calling and the wind has died down and as I take a breath of the finest mountain air, I set my mind to what's needed.

Heading inside, I grab the items needed to cook up some breakfast and then head back outside and start the fire that will help cook the meal. We have a small kitchen inside, but I've always loved eating outdoors. Especially in the cabin. It feels right and so I feel a strange lightness to my spirit as I set about cooking us food and it feels good knowing I'm not alone. If I've brought a woman here before, it's for a quick fuck away from the compound. Living with close on fifty bikers can get a little crowded sometimes. Mind you, I can count on one hand the number of women I've taken away for the night, preferring the solitude a night on my own away from it provides, rather than entertaining someone who doesn't interest me outside of the obvious.

But *she* does. Bonnie Anderson interests me a great deal, and just picturing her sleeping not far away stirs something inside me that's best kept to myself. Desire.

CHAPTER 9

BONNIE

It feels warm, comforting even as the sun's rays hit my face and gently wake me.

Despite everything, I slept well and seeing the sun through the small window tells me I've slept in for a change. Then the events of yesterday come back with a vengeance and I sit up startled back to real life—my life. My twisted, corrupted, tainted life and I'm not out of the woods yet—literally.

Just thinking of what that man did to me yesterday fills me with horror and shame. However, the one emotion that surprises me more is gratitude. He broke the dam that was stifling me and let it all out in one huge crescendo of relief. I needed that. I needed the release and yet I still can't forgive him for what he did.

Gingerly, I dangle my legs over the edge of the bed and decide to have a shower. My limbs ache and my head hurts, probably due to the amount of crying I did last night and I could really use a coffee.

I smell something that makes my stomach growl and as I glance out of the window, I see him in the distance. I hate myself when the sight of his ripped body holds my interest. I detest myself when my gaze lingers on his rock-hard abs as he pokes the fire. Then I feel angry because my body shivers with desire when I see him stretch as he stands up, and my heart races quicker than it should when he runs his hands through the closely cropped hair that makes him even more forbidding.

Yes, I am interested in that man for all the wrong reasons because girls like me don't want men like that. I crave a respectable man, someone with prospects, in a suit preferably; yes, a man who has his shit worked out. Not a tattooed biker from hell who thinks taking out a room of bastards is just another day at the office. Not a man who assaults a woman and thinks nothing of it. Not a man like *him*. But then I remember being held in his arms. The way he comforted me when I lost the plot. The way he felt as I snuggled into that chest and how good it felt. I also bear the imprint of his lips on my cheek, I felt it as he placed me in bed last night. I pretended to be asleep because I didn't know what he would do; it surprised me that he was so gentle. So loving and it felt so good.

Then I remember my humiliation at his hand, and so I grab the nearest clothes I can find and head outside.

It's payback time.

He looks up as I approach and nods, "Morning, darlin', did you sleep ok?"

"Yes, thank you."

The smell coming from the fire is intoxicating, and I realize I haven't eaten since yesterday morning.

"There's coffee brewed and I take mine black."

He winks and carries on frying up his food and I shrug and reach for the pot, pouring him a mug and one for myself.

"Here."

I hand him the coffee and settle down beside the fire he has going and look at him with interest.

"So, what now?"

"We eat."

"And then?"

"Up to you, darlin', the day is ours. We could go for a hike, take a swim, not much else to do."

"You make it sound as if we're on vacation."

"We kind of are."

"Then forgive for not being ecstatic about that because I would much rather go home."

"Are you sure?"

"Of course."

He seems thoughtful, which alarms me a little. "What's the story?"

He grabs a couple of plates and piles them with eggs, bacon and hash browns and says tersely, "What's up, darlin', is that we are stuck here protecting your life until we figure out who wants to take it from you."

My hand shakes as I take the plate.

"Why me?"

He throws me a fork and sits down on the nearby tree stump and shrugs.

"I'm guessing it's someone in your organization. Probably something to do with your undercover operation."

"How do you know this?"

"We have our ways."

As I shovel the food into my mouth, I don't think I've ever tasted anything better, but I'm not going to tell him that. What I want to know more than anything though, is who the fuck wants me dead?

"So, what did they say?"

He shrugs. "That word on the street is someone in the FBI is in heavy with the Knights of Hades. The operation you were running was threatening his or her cover and they were afraid of the information getting out."

"So, someone in my unit?"

I stare at him in horror and he nods. "Probably. The thing

is, we don't know who? All our informant knows is that they were told to get you out of there but had to wait for the signal."

"And they gave it, right?"

I hate the sympathy in his eyes as he shakes his head. "No. It appears that wedding was arranged for one purpose only. To take you out. Blaze knew all along you were undercover and fed you bullshit. Everything you fed back was because he wanted you to. Last night your time had run out because the person controlling his strings was getting antsy."

I feel sick and even my hunger can't stop me pushing the plate away and blinking back the tears. "There's an informant in the FBI, they knew I was going to die."

The sympathy in his eyes is hard to take, and I bite my lip and turn away. Suddenly, everything I believe in means nothing anymore. I feel used, betrayed and so alone I'm glad I'm here because if I was at home, they would probably come for me.

I wasn't aware he had moved until he places his arm around my shoulders and pulls me close, whispering, "I'm sorry, darlin', that can't be easy to hear."

"Why did you save me, what use am I, I know nothing?"

I lift my eyes to his and see a storm approaching. He looks angry and says roughly, "Because there is nothing more we hate as a unit is seeing an innocent person set up. Especially a woman. It ain't right and we act accordingly."

"So, if I was a man, would that have changed things?"

"No. The reason we went in was on the instruction of someone higher up than you, your boss or his boss. Those orders came from the top dog, and what we need to unravel is the mystery surrounding the reason you were there in the first place."

He looks up at the sun and shakes his head. "It's why we're here. Buying time to get to the bottom of the problem and as soon as we have our information, we can set about protecting you and sending you home. Or not."

"Not! What do you mean, not?"

"It may not be safe. You see, you're moving around with a target on your back and I'm your best defense. Sorry to break the bad news, but you had better start trusting me because I'm the only friend you've got right now."

I stare at him in horror and he shrugs before standing and saying over his shoulder.

"Get used to it, darlin' and try to be civil at least. I'm not a patient man as you found out to your cost."

"Oh yes, about that…"

Before he can even turn to look my way, I move quickly and sweep my legs hard in an arc right under his feet and as he falls to the ground, I jump up and straddle him with my knees locked around his neck and my fingers to a pulse point on the side of his head. His grunt of surprise is the only sound he makes as I hiss, "One false move and this pulse stops beating. Now listen hard, never, I repeat never, touch me again, or so help me God, I'll think nothing of repaying the favor."

I almost think he's enjoying this as his mouth twitches and he says darkly, "Don't make promises you can't keep because I'd like to see you try spanking my ass, I might even enjoy it."

I press my finger in deeper and know this particular move can make a grown man shit himself, but to my surprise it only takes him one move and I'm the one lying on my back with him holding both my wrists above my head.

His face hovers dangerously close to mine as he whispers, "Don't play with the bad boys, darlin', we don't have rules. Just accept that I'm a better fighter than you because I've had years of practise."

Bringing my knee up swiftly, I relish the pain in his expression as I make contact with his balls but they must be made of steel because all he does is hiss and growl, "Predictable."

With his hand on my throat, I struggle to breathe as he grabs his belt and tethers my wrists. Then he slings me over his shoulder and grips my ass tightly with one hand.

I struggle and kick out but he is holding me in a way I can't make contact and before I know it, I'm in the cabin, with my back on the bed.

Frantically, I kick out and he just laughs and from out of nowhere, removes handcuffs from thin air and slaps them on my bound wrists before fixing them to the bedpost and then doing the same to my ankles.

My breathing is ragged as he steps back and looks at me with satisfaction, and the bastard actually laughs. "Just how I like them."

The look in his eyes is not a sight I want to dwell on because this man is scaring the shit out of me as he throws me an angry glare and leaves the room, slamming the door behind him. I cry out, "You fucking bastard, untie me."

The only reply I get is the sound of his bike starting up and in total shock I hear him tearing away as if his life depends on it.

CHAPTER 10

SNAKE

God help me, I had to get out of there. The fact she even laid me out was a shock, but when she pulled that pressure point move, I was incensed. She's a fighter, that's for sure and part of me admires her for that. Then again, I'm angry. More at myself than her because she only did what most would do if they had been held against their will. The trouble with me is I'm too nice, and that gets you nowhere except a huge headache that is threatening to send me feral.

I had to leave for her own safety because when I saw her bound at my mercy, I have never wanted anyone as much as I did her.

Just imagining sliding into a little piece of heaven like that has my emotions all over the place. She's wild, I like that. She's beautiful, that goes without saying. In fact, I think she is possibly the most beautiful woman I have ever seen and that attitude, I like that too and I congratulate the gods on finding me my perfect woman. That is why I left, because so help me God, I want that woman so badly it hurts and the only way to guarantee her safety is to place distance between us.

I decide to head into town. There's a bar we use and I could sure use a drink right now. Come to think of it, whoever stocked the cabin is a fucking sadist because there wasn't a drop of the hard stuff anywhere in sight.

I hit the local bar and Elias looks up and grins. "Snake, haven't seen you around here for a while. To what do we owe the pleasure?"

"Business."

He slides me a beer and laughs. "Always business."

He watches as I knock it back and slam the empty on the bar with satisfaction. "I needed that."

"So, how long are you here for?"

I just raise my eyes and stare and he nods. "You got it."

Elias has known The Reapers for longer than I can remember and knows not to ask questions that could get him into trouble. He has always had our backs and we trust him with our lives, which makes him one of a very select club. Like most of our cabins we have a local man who keeps his eye open and his mouth zipped where it concerns us and in this particular town, Elias is that man.

He looks at me thoughtfully, "Do you need company? I can arrange it."

"I'm good thanks."

He refills my glass and I say darkly, "Anything I should know?"

Leaning closer, he whispers, "The town is on a knife edge after the hit on the Knights. They're talking of a dirty war and word is of a rival biker gang rolling into town and trying to take over."

I smirk, "Let them talk."

He chuckles. "There's another rumor it's mafia led. Can you believe it?" He grins, "What would the mafia want in Dusty Springs, these people have overactive imaginations?"

"Then let them. It will settle down and then they'll be onto the next topic of conversation."

Elias looks thoughtful. "So, the Knights have gone, which leaves a gaping hole I'm sure won't take long to fill. My money is on the Devils."

I nod because he's hit the nail on the head. The Red Devils are another gang in town that had nowhere near the contacts the Knights had. Now the coast is clear for them to step up, which suits our purpose because that club is only interested in bikes, sex and drinking. It's possible they could be corrupted and we'll keep an eye on that, but for now this town can sleep safe at night knowing that the cloud they've lived under for far too long now has lifted and sunny days are ahead.

Elias leaves me to it and I think about Bonnie, currently tied up and probably plotting my immediate death when I release her. She interests me a little too much for my liking because I'm not one for tying myself to one woman. It wouldn't be fair on them because of the life I lead. Ryder's much the same, although one overambitious whore tried to trap him into marriage and the result is one gorgeous bundle of trouble who goes by the name of Cassie. Thinking of Ryder's daughter makes me smile because I couldn't love her any harder if she was my own flesh and blood. Despite the fact her mom is dust right now, that little girl gets so much love it's doubtful she will even miss her. I know Ryder worries about that and that worries me because if that man has something on his mind, it usually ends up causing me a massive headache.

Finishing up, I stand ready to leave. I've cooled down enough to return and deal with the shit I've left waiting, and Elias looks up as I slam the dollars on the counter. "On the house."

Shaking my head, I grin. "It's your tip."

He rolls his eyes at the $100 note lying there and I nod. "Usual parting speech."

He nods. "Goes without saying."

As I leave, I think on Elias and smile. I trust him to let me know if anyone comes asking questions and to act as my early warning system. He is good at playing dumb and is assured of his safety by reputation. Anyone messes with him, or any of our caretakers around the states, they get an unwelcome visit from a very surly bunch of bikers who don't have any listening skills. It's their other skills many avoid seeing first hand and so the $100 is well spent on keeping our friends loyal.

Now for my main problem and as I ride back to the cabin, I wonder how I'm gonna approach this. She'll be mad, I kind of understand that, but she needs to know I will not be challenged. Thinking on the ways I usually bring a woman under my control won't work with her, I already know that and I'm not prepared to be that monster, so I'll have to think of another way. Part of me should regret this, regret speaking up and taking Tyson's place, but it was something I had to do. Bonnie Anderson is important to me and now it's up to me to discover why?

CHAPTER 11

BONNIE

I am angry, frustrated and so ashamed I hate the tears that threaten to escape. How does he do this? Humiliate me so easily. First, he spanked me like a child and now this. Chained to the bed like a dog, leaving me to plot revenge in the most destructive of ways. I hate him. More than hate him, detest, dislike, loathe and despise him. I throat punch that part of me that has other ideas about how she feels about him because I can't deal with her now. She's a bitch that has no business being part of me because as soon as he releases me, I'm going down for murder.

You killed a man

Oh yes, I probably am, anyway. The shame is never far away it seems because I have only ended up in this mess because of an even greater one. I murdered a man in cold blood because I am in no doubt about that. I intended on ending Blaze's life, and I swear I see him sitting in the corner of the room looking at me with Karma riding shotgun. I deserve this after what I've done, and I'm in no doubt this is just the tip of the iceberg. Karma is about to seal my fate when the authorities catch up with me and send me to become a permanent wearer of orange when I'm convicted of murder.

I shiver, and it's not because of the cool breeze caressing my body from the open window. It's my own actions that have led me here and not for the first time, I wonder why I couldn't be content with a safe and normal career choice. Why place myself in danger and live on an edge I am deciding I no longer want to be? I want to marry an accountant, or a realtor. Somebody normal who will give me two kids and a nice home on Wisteria Lane. I don't want this. The drama, the anger and the guilt that comes with the badge. I want to rewind time and start again. But I can't. That's pretty obvious right now, so I'll just have to make the best of a bad situation and do what I must to get through whatever this is.

I hear the bike heading back up the track. At least I think it is and wonder about the man who rides it.

I've never met anyone like him before, and I've met many hard-assed bikers and criminals. Is he a criminal? I kind of think he is, but there's something in his eyes that makes me stop and think. A kindness that's at odds with his appearance. Just thinking of him as human almost makes me laugh out loud because this man is a beast of the worst kind. But is he?

The door slams and I prepare myself for another battle and sigh inside. I'm not strong enough. I can't take him on all the time. I'm living under the shadow of what I've done. I need to stop and think for a moment, so as he enters the room, I just stare at him with a dead expression.

"Calmed down yet?"

His voice grates on the one last remaining nerve I have, and I grit my teeth.

"Yes."

He nods and heads across and stares down at me.

"I'll untie you, but before I do, there are a few rules I want you to agree to."

"Ok."

I throw him my blankest look and the bed dips as he sits beside me, taking up most of the space and making my heart race just a little faster with more excitement than I'm happy about.

"Rule 1, no trying to kill your rescuer, not a good way to thank them for their trouble. Rule 2, no backchat unless you want a repeat of yesterday. Rule 3, be civil at least, and pull your weight around here. I'm not your servant and we share the chores. Rule 4, talk to me. Tell me what you know and why you think your unit is out to kill you."

My eyes widen at his last rule and he looks concerned and says a little softer, "Sorry, darlin', it's a fact. They were never coming for you, and we were the only thing standing between you and a violent ending."

I can't help the tear that trickles down my cheek and to my surprise, he reaches out and strokes it lightly away. "Don't cry, darlin', get even. It always works for me."

I nod and then I feel his fingers at my wrists as he gently releases the cuffs before turning his attention to my ankles. I don't react, I don't do anything because I know he is being kind and I'm keen to keep this version of him because kindness will go a long way with me right now and so I just rub my wrists and sniff. "Thank you."

He nods and stands, looking away quickly. "Come, I'll fix you a drink; it's where I've been, gathering the resources we sure need right now."

He laughs as if he's some fucking comedian, and as my legs dangle over the edge of the bed, I take a deep breath. I need to focus, push aside emotion until I'm safe because I'm in danger in every way possible because now the beast has revealed some humanity, that crazy bitch that's attracted to him has risen to the challenge and is pushing away the side of me that hates him with every other part of her rational brain.

I find him in the kitchen pouring two whiskies into small glasses and he offers me one as soon as I head into the room.

"One for medicinal purposes only."

"Thank you."

I take the glass and note he downs his in one and I laugh. "What's your excuse?"

"You."

I can't help but grin and he smiles, which momentarily stuns me. He looks so different, almost human when he smiles. Why do I like this so much?

"So, darlin', how did a pretty girl like you end up undercover in hell?"

The feminist inside me roars at his description, but I save that particular fight for another day. "I always wanted to be a cop. My dad was a cop, and he was the man I looked up to the most. He was always my hero, and I wanted to make him proud."

"And you think becoming a cop did that?"

"Yes, why, don't you?"

"No. If I had a daughter, I would do everything to talk her out of it. It's not a life I want for my pride and joy; couldn't you become a teacher or something, I'm guessing he would be more than proud of you then?"

"Are you seriously saying my dad isn't proud of me?"

I feel my eyes flash and as he looks at his watch, he sighs heavily. "Two minutes. Man, I had hoped for five at least."

"What are you talking about?" My voice is irritable, and he laughs softly. "Before you talked back to me. I had thought we could fall into an easy companionship, but everything I say seems to light the fire inside you. Word of advice, darlin', calm down and don't take everything to heart, I'm not the bad guy here, believe it or not I want to help."

Suddenly, I feel bad. He's right. I've done nothing but talk back, be sarcastic and generally cause him a problem, and because I don't like the way he deals with that, I'm making a bad situation much worse.

Sighing, I smile my apology and he looks a little stunned. "I'm sorry."

He nods and refills his glass and offers me some and as I hold out my glass, he winks. "One more, then we should probably start those chores."

As I down the shot, I feel the warm liquid pushing away the pain and feel a little better about the situation. He's right, he's done nothing but help and I need to remind myself of that even though his caveman attitude doesn't sit well with me. We can work on it though, at least I'm safe—for now, anyway.

CHAPTER 12

SNAKE

She's surprised me. I figured she'd fight like a coyote when I released her but it appears as if all the fight's gone out of her leaving a very desirable woman in its place. When she smiled, it was like a punch to my gut because it disarmed me a little. I've never met a woman like Bonnie. Maybe it's the red hair, so bright it glows like a river of blood. Possibly it's the dark smoldering eyes that are fanned by the darkest, longest lashes I have ever seen, touching her face like feathers, making her seem sultry, mysterious and so damn sexy my cock physically aches. Then there's her porcelain skin as white as snow that has no blemish in sight. Even with no make-up, this woman is so beautiful it hurts to look at her without wanting to touch. Her figure is perfection from the rounded plump tits and tapered waist that swells to rounded hips and a peachy ass. Those long legs would look good around my waist as I push in hard, and as she looks at me with curiosity, I guess her thoughts are of a much darker kind.

She sighs and sets her glass down. "Ok, what do you want me to do?"

Shaking myself, I drive away the image of her on her knees

sucking my cock as the first tick on the to do list and say roughly instead, "You can clean up this cabin while I fetch some more wood. There's some food in the fridge we could eat for lunch."

For once she doesn't come back with some smart-ass comment and just nods as she turns and heads from the room. Once again, I wonder about my sanity in being here in the first place. I don't babysit, I don't have time for that but there's something about this whole situation I'm loving right now and it's because of her, Bonnie Anderson, the cop I should never have met in the first place.

Thinking it's best to create distance—again—I head outside to gather wood for the fire. It's rare that I come here, or to any of our cabins, actually. Mainly I stay at the compound and help Ryder organize the shit we deal with, so it's like being on vacation without the pleasure. I wonder what Bonnie's thinking right now. I'm guessing she's pissed; it hurts her to put up with my shit, I can see that and the cop in her is wary of me. The fact we just murdered a room full of bastards must have her itching to bring us to justice. Then it hits me and I feel like a fool.

She killed a man.

I've grown so used to it I don't think anymore—but her... It's probably her first kill and I hope to God it's the last.

Setting down my ax, I head back inside because she must be dealing with serious shit right now and I was so wrapped up in playing the captor, I forgot to look behind the mask she wears so well.

As soon as I see her standing washing the dishes, I know I was right. She is staring out of the small window and the fact she is washing the same dish over and over again tells me she needs help. She doesn't move, just stares out of the window as if the answer lies there and I move behind her and say gently, "I need you to come outside."

She jumps and looks around and I know I was right. There's a brightness to her eyes that tells me she's struggling, and I'm grateful that she just nods and places the dish on the side.

"Sure."

She follows me out and I think on how to play this. I need to let her talk, purge the memory from her soul, and for a man not used to listening this could be a hard hour ahead.

I guide her to the clearing where I was chopping logs and jerk my thumb toward the fallen tree stump. "Your throne awaits, princess."

She just sits and stares around her with interest and I'm grateful we have a place like this to deal with this shit because with only nature as our companion it will help.

Sitting across from her, I say gently, "Do you wanna talk about what happened with Blaze?"

Immediately her eyes fill and she looks troubled. "I'm not sure if I can."

She looks down and plays with her fingers and I sigh.

"Was he the first man you killed?"

She looks up, startled. "Of course, I don't make a habit of murdering people you know."

"You could have fooled me." I grin to take the sting from my words and she shrugs. "Well, you asked for it."

"So, I'll ask again, do you wanna talk about it? I'm a good listener."

"Are you?"

I nod and she sighs heavily. "It was fight or die; I know that. I'm not stupid, I know what he had planned for me and it wasn't going to be pretty. The trouble is, I can't get the image from my mind of his final look. The way he stared at me with shock, disbelief, and yet an acceptance that he was about to take his last breath. I've never watched a man die from my hand before and I'm not sure I ever want to again."

"Understandable. No one likes to be the person responsible

for ending another human's life, no matter how much they deserve it."

"How do you live with yourself?" Her voice is husky and outlined in desperation, and I shrug. "I cope. I've always coped because I would go mad if I didn't. I tell myself that the people I kill have done worse to other innocent people. I understand that taking them out will make the world a better place and the added sweetener is that usually I rescue someone who can start again."

"Like me."

I nod. "Is that what you want—to start again?"

"How do I know? Yesterday I thought I was doing a responsible job. I was helping bring the bad guys down. Now I'm not so sure who the bad guys are anymore."

"Do you think I'm one of them?"

"Possibly, I'm not sure. I mean, you look bad, scary even." She laughs softly and I shrug. "I get that."

"But something inside me is telling me I'm safe with you despite the fact you've assaulted me twice now and I could have you on a charge for both of them."

"So, sue me."

I grin and as she laughs softly, I love the sound of it.

She fixes me with a curious look. "So, what brought you to the gates of Hades? You say you were under instruction, from who?"

"Someone higher up than your boss. A department who has put yours under investigation. The investigators being investigated, that's pretty fucked up, wouldn't you say?"

"I guess."

She looks a little uncertain and then decides to go there, anyway. "So, The Twisted Reapers. Tell me about them."

"Darlin', you wouldn't believe me if I did. No, when you learn about the Reapers, it will be by experience rather than words."

"What do you mean?" She looks afraid and I smile. "When I take you there, you'll see first-hand."

"When you take me there. What do you mean?"

Standing, I cover the distance between us and drop to my knees before her, fixing her with a look that shocks even me. "When I take you home."

She bites her lip and looks anxious. "But I don't live there."

"You will."

She looks scared shitless and I laugh softly. "I'm guessing you think I'm crazy, but I see things very clearly. Once we discover who's setting you up, you won't want to return to your old job."

"What if I do?"

Her eyes flash and I love how magnificent she looks. "Because the trust has gone. You will always remember they sacrificed you to keep a secret they hoped would never come out. You will think you can continue but the first job you go on you will be questioning it. You will never feel comfortable again and it will destroy you from the inside."

"What are you, a fortune teller or something?"

"Don't need to be. I know your future, Bonnie, even if you don't. I saved you and now you belong to me—period."

She flinches as if my words hit her hard and whispers, "I belong to you, what are you talking about?"

To be honest, I think I'm crazy myself right now because this is new territory for me, but I think I've known since we laid eyes on her when Blaze dragged her to his side. The fact I couldn't wait to step in and save her before things got out of hand. The fact I nearly defied my own fucking President and went in anyway told me she was special and she is. Bonnie Anderson is going to be my old lady, and she doesn't even know it yet. Luckily, I do, and so I'm taking this time to convince her that she wants it too.

CHAPTER 13

BONNIE

What the hell was in that drink because this man is talking in riddles? Why wouldn't I go back to work if I was able to? It's my job, my occupation, the thing I've worked so hard to get. Go home with him to a biker's fuck palace. I know what it's like, hell I've watched the Knights for close on two weeks already and was only saved from being one of their fuck buddies by the man who wanted me for himself. Blaze. Now I think on it, I know this man is right. Blaze knew who I was all along, and if he did, someone in my department told him.

I feel cold and shiver a little, and I'm surprised when a strong arm reaches out and wraps me into a hard chest. Rather than pull away, I allow myself the comfort he brings and love the smell of safety. I know I'm safe with him don't ask me how, I just do.

"What's your name?"

The words tumble from my lips borne out of curiosity and he says in a husky voice, "Snake."

"That figures, I'm guessing your parents didn't name you that at birth, so what's the story?"

Pulling back, I try to switch the topic of conversation onto safer ground and decide to find out as much as I can about the man who rattles my hormones so badly.

"He pulls me down beside him and we sit looking out across the forest and he says huskily, "A snake saved my life, I felt I owed it."

"How?"

He laughs softly. "I was on assignment in the jungle in southern Asia. I was hunting a group responsible for kidnapping a scientist, and our intelligence led us to an area in the deepest part of the jungle. Our instructions were to stake it out, lie low and observe. I did as I was told and must have been there for two days before it happened."

"What?" I am mesmerized because just thinking of what this man has lived through is fascinating the hell out of me and I shiver as I see the tattoo of a cobra winding its way around his arm, its head drifting toward his neck.

"My only companion was the cobra who was watching from a nearby tree. I couldn't shoot it; I was performing a covert operation and any sound would alert my targets. I kept my eye on him though, and we shared that at least."

I shiver just imagining it and wonder how he could have kept his cool in that situation.

"We struck up quite a friendship because he seemed to accept my company and after a while I wasn't bothered. Until…"

He breaks off and I feel a shiver down my spine as I sense the bite in the tail coming.

"It was dusk, and I was getting pissed by now. I'm not one to lie around all day and it was getting uncomfortable. I wasn't alone, though. I was part of a unit doing the same as me around the perimeter of the camp, but it was hard. Just watching, waiting, and not even being able to take a piss standing up."

"You mean…"

My eyes are wide as he laughs. "Yes, darlin', sometimes you just need to give control over to nature and worry about it another day. Anyway, I took to watching the cobra, studying it and getting acquainted with it. It surprised me when it moved toward me, and yet I held back. I recognized the type, A King Cobra whose venom could kill a man inside of fifteen minutes after paralyzing him first. However, I knew they are shy and usually avoid humans, so when it came to say hi, I thought it had a change of heart."

"Were you afraid?"

I can't begin to imagine anything scaring this man, and to my surprise he nods. "Yes, I was afraid. I'm not stupid enough not to respect nature. I know how cruel she can be, and yet I know animals don't kill for fun either. I was no threat, no bother to that snake, and yet something brought it to me and that intrigued me more than anything."

I shiver and he laughs, pulling me closer and whispering, "Spoiler alert—I lived to tell the tale."

Despite myself, I laugh and then say with interest, "So, what happened next?"

"It turns out I wasn't the target."

"An animal?"

"You could call him that."

He laughs. "One of the kidnappers had found my position and was creeping up on me. He was obviously good too because I never heard a thing. Luckily for me the cobra decided he wasn't bored with me yet and the first I knew about my imminent death was when the snake shot past me and I heard a scream."

"You must have been so scared."

I stare at him in awe and he looks at me with a strange expression before nodding. "I was. My first reflex was to revert to training and as I rolled to the side aiming my gun upward, I saw the man clutching his eyes and screaming before shaking and falling down onto the jungle floor. The cobra took up residence on his body and I stared in surprise as it looked back at me and something about the way it looked me right in the eye, made me feel an emotion I have never felt before. It saved me, I know that for a fact, and maybe it was the disturbance, or the scream that made the decision for us, I got the call to go in and take the bastards out. I never saw the snake again, so I had a permanent reminder tattooed on my arm. Two warriors sharing the same space, and my solider in arms."

Weirdly I find his tale so emotional the tears trickle down my face and he laughs softly, "Hey baby, it's a happy story, why the tears?"

He uses his thumb to wipe them away and as his skin makes contact with mine, I hitch my breath and stare into his eyes that pull me in deep.

For a second, we just stare, both balancing on the edge of something that could destroy us both, and yet I still lift my hand and trace the tattoo with a reverence that I feel deep in my soul. Snake looks at me with an intense desire that I recognize because for some reason I am experiencing the same. Why do I want him so badly when he's so crude and caused me pain and humiliation? Then again, he saved me, he brought me here to keep me safe, and that's a powerful enough reason to lean in and touch his lips lightly with mine.

To my surprise, he pulls back a little and traces a path down my face with his finger and whispers, "When I take you home, Bonnie, you will not want to be anywhere else."

"What if I don't want to go?"

"You will."

I think I physically ache for him to touch me, wrap me up in those strong arms and keep the world outside, but I know this is just a reaction to my situation, so I pull away and look down. "I'll fix us some lunch; you must be hungry."

He says nothing as I stand and walk away, feeling slightly lost as I create distance between us. Why do I want him so badly? I've fallen into madness, that can be the only explanation but I do, want him that is, it's whether I want him to keep me that the jury's still undecided on.

CHAPTER 14

SNAKE

I feel the frustration tearing me from the inside. I want her so badly, but I'm not about to scare her off either. Like the cobra Bonnie is curious and shy with a deadly bite and I need to earn her trust first. It would have been so easy to lean in and taste those lips that I will dream of tonight. So easy to lay my claim to a woman I already know is mine. But she would hate me tomorrow, and then herself. She's not ready for me yet, and I already know I will take as long as it takes to make her mine.

I carry on chopping the wood and think about the cobra from my past. I owe him my life; I know that for a fact and the snake settles my nerve in battle knowing I have the ultimate protector by my side. I have the cobra on one side and Ryder on the other, so my safety is guaranteed. The King Cobra, two dark entities protecting my life and now I just need Bonnie and my life will be complete. But first we need to mend her like only we can–only *I* can and so with a sigh and yet a heart full of resolution, I head inside to help with lunch.

She nods toward the fridge and says evenly, "Take the salad and meat outside, I'll being the drinks and bread."

I do as I'm told and I love how this feels. Like we're a unit of our own, a family. My only family that counts is my military one that is disguised by leather and whispered rumors. The Twisted Reaper MC. A band of ex-military assassins paid to do the government's dirty work and paid well as it happens. We fight, plot and end lives and all in the name of duty on the streets of America. Not the jungle, not the desert, and not in hostile foreign territory. I love my life but I need more and that's where Bonnie comes in. She will fill the void that's growing larger every second I worry she won't agree. Now I just need to convince her to stay.

She is quiet through lunch and I try to get her to open up a little. "So, tell me about your father, he sounds a great guy."

Her eyes shine as she smiles. "He is. A hero, in fact. He always was to me and mom and I was so proud when he came to my graduation ceremony. I wanted to be the best—for him."

"He must be proud."

"He is, but then I'm guessing he wouldn't be so proud if he knew what I'd done."

"He would be prouder."

"What makes you say that?" She hangs onto my every word and my gut wrenches as I sense how much her father's approval means to her. "Because you are one of the best, Bonnie. Fearless, drenched in desire to succeed and not afraid to do what you must to bring the bad guys down. Not many women would put themselves in your position. It's just a miracle you escaped intact because I've seen some horrific things these bikers do their captives and make no mistake, you were their captive. It's only the fact they knew who you were that bought you time, but ultimately you were in for a horrific ending."

Her eyes fill with tears and she nods. "I know."

"Then hold your head up with pride and know you did what you had to survive. Think about those other women who weren't so lucky and if you want justification for what you did, picture their souls in heaven way earlier than they should have been. You saved many other women by bringing him down, so don't you let him inside your head."

"But you would have finished him off, I didn't need to kill him."

I watch the tears spill down her face and growl, "True, but anything could have happened, a hesitation on our part, if he had an idea and used you as a shield, you just don't know how the story could have ended, so you did what you had to do. Park that emotion and leave it behind you because he doesn't deserve another thought in your pretty little head."

She laughs and says in a hard voice, "Could you spout any more macho bullshit if you tried?"

"Not where it concerns you, darlin', I'm straight out of the cave."

She laughs, and it settles my soul. Thank God.

We finish up and the food tastes even better because she prepared it. I'm loving just looking at her and can't imagine how I'd feel if I held her in my arms, skin on skin.

I also love the way she looks at me when she thinks I'm not watching. Small glances of interest that cause her skin to heat and make her look away quickly. I know she is more interested in me than she would like known and I decide to use that to my advantage.

Ripping off my t-shirt, I flex my muscles and sigh. "Man, this is hot. Fancy a dip?"

The fact her eyes are fixed straight on my torso makes me feel like the cocky bastard I am as she says with distraction, "Yes… it is a little hot."

Standing, I hold out my hand and say quickly, "There's a lake through the trees, we should cool off."

"But I don't have a costume."

"Neither do I." I wink and add, "I won't tell if you won't."

"What, skinny dip?"

Her eyes are wide with horror and I nod. "Yes, darlin', nature is calling, can't you hear her cry?"

She blushes as deep as her hair color and yet she takes my hand and as my hand curls around hers, I feel a connection so deep it's like my whole life flashes before my eyes.

We walk silently to the lake that glistens through the trees as we approach and she gasps, "It's beautiful."

"It sure is." I stare at her the whole time and once again she blushes before I laugh and lower my pants, revealing nothing but a very interested cock pointing in her direction.

She steps back a little in shock and I laugh and dive straight in shouting, "Your turn."

She looks around her nervously and I almost think she'll bale out, but then she tilts her heat in defiance and I swear I stop breathing as she lifts the t-shirt over her head and steps out of the cargo pants she seems attached to.

Standing before me in nothing but her underwear, she seems more vulnerable and yet so fierce it brings a smile to my face.

There she is, my warrior queen, and I have never seen anything so beautiful in my life.

CHAPTER 15

BONNIE

I can't believe I'm doing this. I'm stripping in the open air with a man who scares the shit out of me watching. Just thinking of what he could do to me, has done already, makes me throb with a primal reaction I am finding hard to ignore. He's so dangerous, a predator. A man of duty and yet a renegade. I love the dark side of him that dominates. I love the caring side of him that comforts and I adore his quick wit and no-nonsense attitude and to hell with the consequences. I may be going down for murder, so I may as well live while I can.

So, with a wicked attitude, I remove my underwear slowly and seductively, holding his attention with my eyes. I'm not sure when I became so devilish. Maybe it's when my life flashed before my eyes back at the Knights of Hades' clubhouse. Maybe I need this to distract me from a problem I can't seem able to deal with, so without care I dive into the water and relish the cool crystal water welcoming me inside.

As I surface, I focus and see Snake treading water a short distance away, watching me through a predator's eyes and a delicious shiver runs through me. I'm interested in discovering more about this man. He's an enigma but there is something so comforting about having him beside me and as our eyes connect, I can see he feels the same. He's holding back, probably out of fear of yet another attempt by me to end his life but I'm done with fighting; I'm done with trying to escape because I am coming to the conclusion that I am safer *with* him rather than without him.

I swim across and smile.

"This feels so good."

"I thought we could use it; things have been a little intense and I'm done with that."

"Me too." I smile and love the desire that lights in his eyes as he watches me. He may scare the shit out of me, but I want him so badly I surprise myself when I whisper, "So, what now?"

The fact we are both naked doesn't concern me as he shifts a little closer.

"What do you want to happen?"

"A race maybe?"

If I could punch myself right now, I would. A fucking race, am I an idiot? A strong, sexy, gorgeous man is standing before me offering me anything I want and I choose a fucking race.

Despite how annoyed I am right now—at myself, I laugh and break away. "First one to that tree over there gets to choose their prize."

Taking a deep breath, I start to swim and thank my parents for the lessons they made me go to as a child. The thought there may be snakes or alligators in this lake doesn't even concern me because I am so high on adrenalin, I just set off intent on winning.

To my surprise, I'm the first one there and I watch as Snake follows close behind and I smirk.

"I win."

Something in his expression tells me I was always going to and as the bastard smirks and says, "You sure did." I know it was by choice—his.

Treading water, I say triumphantly, "So, I get a prize."

"What's it to be?"

He looks interested and I feel a little heated thinking about what I really want. Actually, I want it more than anything right now, so before I can change my mind I say slightly breathlessly, "I want you to kiss me."

I'm sure my cheeks must be flaming brighter than my hair right now as he looks surprised. "A kiss, that's shocked me."

"Has it?" I feel a little unsure now. Maybe I read the signals wrong as he shakes his head. "For a woman who has done everything possible to get out of here, I thought you'd ask for that. Then again, maybe that's still your plan and one kiss from you would seal my fate."

We share a grin as I laugh, "Like a praying mantis."

"Something like that."

I edge a little closer and he watches me with interest. I'm guessing he's used to this. Women wanting him and not being afraid to do anything to get what they want, but I'm not one of them—normally that is. Hell, I can't even remember the last time I got laid, it's been so long, which is maybe why I'm feeling so desperate now.

He holds my eyes with his and says huskily, "Should I be afraid right now?"

"You—afraid, I doubt that ever happens."

He smirks and nods. "Would it shock you if I said I was?"

"Of me."

He nods.

"Why?"

"Because I'm in unfamiliar territory and one false move could ruin everything."

"Ruin what?"

I'm genuinely confused, and he inches a little closer and his voice is a whisper on the breeze as he says, "Ruin *us*, you see, Bonnie, you may be surprised at this but I chose to bring you here. It was always meant to be Tyson, but I couldn't bear the thought of it."

"Tyson?" I am genuinely confused, and he takes another step and says, "Another Reaper at the clubhouse. He was to bring you here to keep you safe until Ryder discovers who wants you dead. Then I saw you and everything changed for me. You see, that first look told me one thing I still don't understand now."

"What?" I feel breathless as he closes the gap and stands inches away. "That you and me were destiny waiting to play her trump card, the winning hand, you see, Bonnie, when I saw you standing there, I knew you belonged with me."

I am stunned, genuinely stunned, because the look in his eyes tells me he means every word. It's as if he has drawn back a curtain and revealed the picture behind because I see it clearly too. A future with this man, don't ask me how, I just know and it's as if our worlds collide in this moment and fate walks away with a smile on her face at a job well done. Snake and Bonnie, for some reason I know it was written in the stars.

My insides are a mess of emotions right now and the only release is to claim my prize, so I close the gap and reaching up, run my hand around the back of his head and pull it down to mine, fastening my lips on his in a moment of reckoning. As they touch, it feels so good and as I kiss Snake, I feel my heart jump with relief. He tastes of everything I ever wanted and more besides. He tastes of new beginnings and hope and he tastes of destiny—mine, so I pull him closer and show him just how much I want him because if this bastard is playing me, I suck at life.

CHAPTER 16

SNAKE

I let her win and I feel as if I just got first prize. It was always going to be Bonnie's decision to make because if it takes me weeks, months, years even, I was always going to keep her until she never wanted to leave. Now she is kissing me and it's not enough. It will never be enough because until I have explored every inch of this beautiful woman a million times, I won't be content. Hell, I doubt I'll even be content then because Bonnie is the life in my veins that enables me to live. I knew that as soon as she pressed those plump lips to mine and allowed me inside. This kiss is the first and feels like it. I've kissed many women before, but it's as if this is the first time it ever had meaning. She tastes so sweet, like the finest delicacy that makes you greedy for more, but I have to let her call the shots. I can't ruin this by going in too strong because given half a chance I would be inside her right now. It's why I let her win. I knew what I would ask for and it's this— one kiss with her. But it would have felt wrong, as if I was taking something I didn't deserve, so I waited for her to reach my page, want me as much as I want her, and it didn't take long.

Just feeling her wet tits pressed against my chest makes me feral and as she wraps her tongue around mine, it tastes like heaven. Just imagining how I'll feel when I'm inside her makes me impatient but I'm not pushing her too far, it's at Bonnie's pace, not mine and I am fast realizing this is the hardest battle I will ever face - her.

She moans against my mouth and my cock presses hard against her pussy and she rubs on it suggestively as the water laps around us. As kisses go, this one lasts longer than most because it appears she's in no hurry to stop. Her hands move to my back and she grinds against me, making me almost come on the spot, then she pulls back and the wild look in her eyes that are heavy with desire, tell me everything I need to know.

"Thank you." She whispers the word and looks at me with a flush to her beautiful cheeks, and her breathing is heavy. I feel my own is erratic and for the first time in my life I'm not sure what to do next.

Then she surprises me again by stepping closer and whispering, "I don't think I'm done with you yet."

Once again, she pulls my head down and rubs her body against mine and I groan, "You taste so good, are you sure you want this, darlin'?"

I have to know because this could escalate real fast and she says with a catch to her voice, "Please don't make me beg."

Wrapping my arm around her waist, I draw her in closer and she shivers against me and not from the cool water that dances around us, catching the sunlight, making it feel as if fireworks are exploding everywhere.

This time I show Bonnie just how a man kisses the woman he chooses to be his, and I hold on tight and devour that pretty little mouth that makes me hard just thinking about it.

She groans as I rest my hands on her ass and pull her in hard against my rock-hard cock. Her breath hitches as she says with an urgency that makes me smile, "It's not enough."

"So greedy, baby."

I laugh against her lips and she reaches down and cups my balls and squeezes gently, causing me to bite her lip in surprise. Then she jumps and wraps her legs around my waist and just feeling her pussy grinding against my cock makes any sane decision leave me in an instant.

"I want you inside me, Snake."

If I am surprised, I'll park it for another day because any restraint I had has been cut free by her words, so with a growl, I lift her ass and lower her onto my throbbing cock and as she slides on home, it feels like the biggest victory of my life. She gasps and I love the wild look in her eyes as she pulls back and stares deep into mine. With her legs wrapped around my waist and me buried deep inside her, she smiles and presses her lips to mine, whispering, "That feels so good."

As I lift her hips gently and thrust inside, she stares deep into my eyes the whole time. We are connected in every way possible and it feels like a life changing moment. I'm not fucking Bonnie, I'm delivering a promise. She's mine and that's for life. A connection so strong it hit me hard across the room the moment I laid eyes on her and as we cement the deal, it never felt so good.

She bites her lip and rides my cock and I am happy to do this all day because I know that as soon as I leave her, I'll want to return and as her tits rub against my chest, I don't think I've ever been so happy.

She throws her head back and screams as she orgasms hard on my cock and just feeling her throbbing and squeezing me makes me groan as I pull her quickly off and come so hard, it feels as if I will fill the lake with my sperm.

She giggles as I cling on tight, her legs still wrapped around me as I growl, "Fuck that was good—close but good."

The fact we never used a condom should fill me with horror, but it doesn't. It would have ruined the most special moment of my life because I needed to feel all of her, every fucking part of the woman I know fate had marked off her list for me and the fact I've never been with a woman bare back before makes this even more special.

To my surprise, she strokes my tattoo lightly and whispers, "I can see why the snake protected you. Animals have a sixth sense, they know when something is good, something is right and not to mess with what nature intended."

I let her speak and every word lights a flame inside me as she whispers, "You have charmed me too. How do you do that, it's as if nothing else matters but you?"

She looks up and the wonder in her eyes makes me feel so unworthy it likes a punch to my gut. I am a cold-blooded killer, and yet she sees beyond that. She sees *me*, the man inside who only wants the love of a good woman as payback for a life spent protecting others.

Reaching down, I run my thumb across those plump lips and love the desire that is heavy in her eyes. "You're my woman, Bonnie, I think I knew that sooner than you and it's impossible to fight what was written in the stars."

She shivers against me and I sweep her up into my arms effortlessly as if she is a delicate feather. "Come on, let's go and warm up. No regrets."

She strokes my face lightly. "Never where it concerns you."

Once again, I capture those lips and groan, knowing that as soon as we reach that cabin, I am exploring every inch of this woman who has trapped my soul.

CHAPTER 17

BONNIE

If I stopped to think about what I've just done, I would be horrified at myself. How could I give myself up so easily to him - a biker? A rough, sexy as fuck biker who is no doubt carving another notch into his bedpost as he looks on the horizon for the next in line.

I should be ashamed of myself, but for some strange reason I don't care. It feels liberating in fact to do something alien to me. Drag myself out of my comfort zone into a place I wouldn't go if my rational mind was in charge.

I wanted him so badly I couldn't think of anything else and when he entered my body, it was because I wanted him there and now being held so tenderly in his arms, it just makes me want more.

He carries me over to the edge and lifts me carefully to the side, making sure to deposit me on a smooth rock. Then my mouth waters as he drags himself out of the lake, and the water rolls off his glistening muscles as he reveals the impressive beast that I just let into my most guarded place.

His body is absolutely huge and so impressive my mouth waters. I am blinded by lust because I have never even imagined a man like him in my life and I have done the unthinkable, what most parents warn their daughters from doing almost as soon as they have the ability to listen - *I let a man fuck me with no protection who I have only just met.*

Well, lock me up and throw away the key because I'm only human after all and if this man never looks at me again, I will carry this to the grave and wrap myself in the memory on a cold, dark night to treasure as the moment I lost my mind over a man.

He reaches out and takes my hand and says gently, "Come on, darlin', I haven't finished with you yet."

I swear my whole body contracts with a delicious shiver as I imagine what comes next. Fuck, I'll deal with my conscience and all the guilt it throws at me tomorrow because I will not deny myself this moment for all the money in the world.

We grab our clothes but remain naked and stroll back to the cabin hand in hand and I couldn't care less. It feels so liberating and I'm loving the sense of abandon I feel holding Snake's hand. It's wicked, dirty, and I should feel ashamed of myself - but I don't. I'm loving it, so I concentrate on my breathing as I anticipate the pleasure I'm about to receive in the very foreseeable future.

I follow him to the cabin and only the sound of nature welcomes us as the sun beats down on my back and warms my already heated skin.

Snake opens the door and growls, "You still ok with this, darlin'?

I nod, not trusting my own voice right now and as he turns and looks at me, I see the storm in his eyes. "I need to hear you say it."

Swallowing hard, I nod. "Yes, I want this, Snake."

He visibly relaxes and takes my hand and leads me through to the bedroom where the bed looks inviting and I can only imagine the pleasure I'm about to experience between those sheets.

We reach the edge and to my surprise, he drops to his knees and presses a light kiss to my stomach. It feels even more intimate if that's possible, quite humbling as he kneels before me. He breathes in deep and whispers, "I'm taking this slow and if you want me to stop at any time, tell me."

I don't have the power of speech right now if I wanted it and a low moan escapes in place of words.

He laughs softly and as my legs shift a little apart, he helps them on their way and buries his face deep in my pussy. As I feel his soft kisses and gentle licks, I hold my breath and as he bites my clit gently, I close my eyes as I feel such exquisite pleasure, I can't concentrate on anything other than what he's doing where few have been before.

It's almost too much as he samples something there should be laws against and then as I shiver with desire, he presses his lips further up my body until he claims my lips once again and I taste my arousal on his tongue.

His groans are my victory dance, and I am keen to repay the favor and pull back a little before dropping to my knees. He hisses as I take his velvet shaft in my hand and gently rub, causing him to groan out loud. Then I cup his balls and let it slide to the back of my throat, and I swear my mouth has never been so full. As I feel him shake, it brings me more joy than I ever thought possible and I pull him deeper and squeeze tighter as he fucks my mouth.

I almost think it's all over as he groans so loud it's as if he's in pain and then two strong arms lift me up and he plunders my mouth so deep and so hard it's as if he's swallowing me whole.

The urgency increases in the room as he growls and pushes me back on the bed and places both hands either side of my head and looks deep into my eyes.

"Are you sure about this?"

"For fuck's sake, do you need a written invitation?"

I laugh softly and his breath hitches and I see an urgency in his eyes that tells me how much he wants this.

With one powerful thrust he is inside me and just feeling him there makes me lose my mind a little. This feels so good, so life changing as he drives into me, claiming my soul, mating like a wild animal as it conquers its mate.

The bed moves as his enormous frames engulfs mine, and the only sound is the squeaking bed springs and the headboard hitting the wall. It's so primitive, so carnal and so damned amazing I couldn't stop if I tried. Just feeling him inside me makes my soul shatter as I cling onto a moment I am unlikely to get again. Feeling him slide against my walls renders me his biggest fan as I rake his back with my nails and bow down to my master. At this moment, he is just that. The powerful master that is dominating my spirit because I would do anything he asked right now, which tells me I am fucked in more ways than one.

As he continues to dominate me inside, he reaches down and flicks my clit and I swear I see stars. I scream so god damned hard the birds fly from the trees and as I feel the waves of repeating orgasm blinding me to life outside him, I am ruined for any other man. His own roar tells nature not to interrupt and to take the week off because her work is done. She has played a blinder because ecstasy like this can never be repeated as we join our bodies in one slick sheen of sweat. His seed coats my soul and leaves its mark, and I couldn't care less what happens next because being claimed by this man in the most basic of ways is absolutely fine by me.

By the time our breathing evens out and our hearts stop jumping all over the place, it leaves a calm after the storm. Snake rolls off me and tucks me in tight by his side, and it feels so right it cannot possibly be wrong.

I gently stroke his rock-hard abs and love the detail of his tattoos. They are so intricate and I'm sure tell a chilling story and only his labored breathing tells me I'm affecting him.

"What's your real name?"

I'm curious and he laughs. "Well, it's certainly not Snake, I told you how I earned that call sign."

"So, you were in the military. Tell me why?"

"It's what I always wanted to do. I lived a normal life with two parents who provided a loving home along with two brothers. One of them, Jack, went on to become a cop and Joseph turned to the books and became an accountant."

Just thinking of him living a normal life like most of the population seems wrong somehow, and I laugh. "Is something amusing you, darlin'?"

"A little, I just can't imagine you in suburbia, it doesn't seem right somehow."

"I'm sorry I don't have a sorry tale to feed you, what can I say, fate dealt me a low blow?"

I find myself laughing happily and he stills a little and then says with emotion lacing his words, "You should laugh more often, darlin', it's like an angel's song."

This time I laugh out loud. "Listen to you, what would your brothers say if they could hear you now?"

He laughs, and for a moment everything seems normal in a very abnormal situation.

Rolling over, I look into his eyes and say with interest.

"So, why the military?"

"Why not? I like fighting, I like guns, and I hate people who hurt innocent ones. I enlisted and soon made it to special forces, Navy SEALS. It's where I met Ryder, the president of the Twisted Reapers."

I fall silent because this is one story I am keen to hear, and he smiles telling me his memories are happy ones.

"Ryder was my partner in crime throughout our whole

military life. He saved my ass more times than I can count, and I returned the favor. So many times we almost met the grim reaper and when we left, it was to carry on under the radar."

"What do you mean, what do you do now except shoot a roomful of menace dead in a blaze of gunfire?"

He shakes his head and looks a little worried if I'm honest and says gruffly, "Sorry, darlin', I can't speak about the Reapers. Like I said before, you will only find out if you make it your home."

I roll off him and feel so desperate. His words have brought back our situation, and I feel cheated already. I know this is a fleeting moment of pleasure because if I'm going anywhere, it's back to my job, my own unit and my own life where normal people go about their business.

But he won't be there.

I feel as if I've lost something before it was even mine, and so I quickly change the subject. "So, I repeat, what's your real name?"

"Jason."

We both laugh out loud and I grin. "I see a J pattern forming in your family. I can see why you changed it; Snake is much more fitting."

He shifts, and this time stares into my eyes and I see the darkness enter his.

"Come home with me, Bonnie, live with the Reapers - with me. The thought of you going back to them - it hurts me."

"What do you mean, hurts you?"

He sighs heavily. "I know what the bastards you work for are like. Hell, they even sacrificed you for their own selfish reasons. You won't be safe back there and I can offer you safety and a home where no harm will ever come to you."

"And my job, what about that?"

He shakes his head. "There is no job."

CHAPTER 18

SNAKE

The shock in her eyes makes me feel like the biggest bastard in the world as she says with a stutter, "No, job, what are you talking about, of course I still have my job?"

Regretting even bringing it up, I have brought the mistrust back into her eyes and the atmosphere reverts back to the edgy one of before.

Choosing my words carefully, I say with regret, "Your job was gone the moment you stepped inside the gates of Hades. You see, whoever sent you there thought you would never return. They were banking on it because you weren't sent there for the reasons you thought."

"Then why was I sent there?"

I can tell she doesn't believe me and I wonder if I should even be telling her but she needs to know because she has a few hard decisions to face and what better time than holed up here in the mountains to give her a clearer outlook on her future.

"The person who arranged it always wanted you removed. The FBI has a file as big as War and Peace on the Knights and could have gone in and arrested them years ago. Ask yourself what they needed to know so badly they would send a beautiful young woman into the pit of hell?"

I see her mind working overtime and I'm glad about that because Bonnie will need her training to come to terms with this.

"I thought they were planning something big, something that would give us information about their suppliers, contacts, someone we didn't know about."

"And did you?"

She looks thoughtful and chews on her bottom lip, making this a very difficult conversation already. Shifting to conceal what that does to me, I try to focus my mind on business rather than what I really want to be doing right now.

"I found out a lot."

"Are you sure, I mean, they may have been feeding you stuff they wanted you to know? Remember, they knew who you were, and they were playing with you."

Bonnie looks destroyed, I can see it in her eyes and she shakes her head. "But…"

I take her hand and pull her against me, dropping my arm around her shoulder and pulling her tight by my side where she belongs. "You see, darlin', the person who wanted you dead knew this would be the perfect cover."

"But why? I haven't done anything or discovered anything to give them a reason to want me dead—whoever they are?"

She shakes a little and I wrap my arm a little tighter around her and hope my next words don't hurt too much.

"No, you've done nothing but your father has."

She pulls away in shock and I see the pain in her eyes that causes my resolve to harden. I will get her through this if it kills me trying.

"My father." I hate the panic in her eyes and say as evenly as I can, "Your father has upset someone extremely powerful who is out for revenge. You are that revenge, Bonnie."

"Me?"

She shakes a little and I can tell she's struggling, so I give her the hard facts. "Listen, you won't like this story, but it will make you understand why this has happened."

"Just tell me."

She looks at me with a hard expression and I almost regret mentioning it because this could change everything. Then again, in order to keep Bonnie, I may have to lose her first.

"The woman who set you up is your father's mistress."

Her hand flies to her mouth and her eyes brim with tears. Shaking her head, she whispers, "You're lying."

"I'm not."

I stare at her with a blank expression and wonder when my life got so complicated.

"That woman is the one who sent you to Hades, to Blaze and was the person who has been working with the Knights for more years than is acceptable."

"Who?"

Her eyes are so full of hurt and devastation I feel my own heart breaking for her because I know she idolizes her father, but this is a story she needs to hear to understand how serious this is.

"It's been going on for years. Your father worked with her several years ago, which is where they met. He was married at the time, and I believe you were around three or four."

She looks down and I see her digging her nails into her leg to keep herself together and I carry on just desperate to get this over with. "We know this because for several months we have been tapping her phone after we were brought in to monitor her movements."

She looks up in surprise and I quickly carry on before she starts questioning me on the job we do.

"We discovered their affair and heard their conversations. She was getting desperate and told your father she had made it so you had a good job, had promoted you above your counterparts and it still wasn't enough. She was angry and your father was backtracking really fast, which only meant he was never going to leave your mom. So, darlin', one of life's lessons coming up, a woman scorned is a dangerous one because she intended on hurting him where it would cut the most."

"Me." Her voice sounds so sad, devastated and ruined, and I park any sympathy I have for her and nod. "Yes, you. She was going to pay him back for a wasted life, waiting for him to leave you and your mom and move in with her. She placed you with the Knights of Hades by way of retribution and then fed the information back to them. They knew who you were all the time, and she was aware that you would never make it out of there alive. Your father would have no excuses left and would either leave your mom, or she would have her revenge. Either way, she wins."

"That's disgusting."

Bonnie looks sick and I shrug. "We're not dealing with a rational person here, and it was lucky our intel had brought us sniffing around."

"Who sent you?"

"Someone higher up than her. She didn't know, but one of the bikers in the club was also an undercover operative. He was feeding back intel to a different division and discovered her involvement with Blaze. Apparently, he had something on her and used it to his advantage."

"Blackmail."

"Yes, darlin', Blaze was playing the FBI, which was why he survived as long as he did. The men at the top took a while to discover something didn't add up, and when they sent in one of their own, he soon uncovered a spider's web of secrets. Then you arrived."

"Who was it?"

"Not telling, but you weren't the only operative we were

sent in to save that night. The club was to be taken out, and both operatives removed, so the woman in the frame thought she had been successful. Her dirty secret was washed clean with no survivors and she could ride off into the sunset with the man she loved when he had no excuses left."

"Oh my god, do my parents think I'm dead?"

Bonnie looks destroyed and I nod. "I expect so."

She jumps up, "Enough of this shit, I'm going home. I need to see them."

Shaking my head, I say as gently as I can, "You can't. The other operative is being debriefed and until we have enough information to bury her, she must think her plan has worked."

"But…"

"I'm sorry, Bonnie, this is bigger than you, your parents and all of us. We need to sit tight and wait for the all clear and only then will you be reunited with your parents."

"But I can't bear to think of them grieving for me when there is no need."

"I'm sorry, she needs to think she's won."

Bonnie pulls away and says tightly, "This whole situation is one big pile of shit. I want to at least call them, let them know I'm safe and not to worry."

"If you do that, she will know. I'm guessing she is monitoring your father's calls just in case."

"A message then, can't someone tell them I'm ok?"

"No."

I feel a surge of sympathy for Bonnie, but I know a war often makes for hard battles beforehand. She will be reunited with her folks but not until it's safe to do so and if I have to chain her to the bed once again to keep her here, so help me, I will.

CHAPTER 19

BONNIE

I am destroyed. My life has altered after one conversation and made it a lie waiting to unravel. My father has been having an affair almost all my life and I can't even begin to get my head around that. Just thinking of my dear sweet mom and how happy I always thought they were, makes my blood run cold. Snake must be wrong; their intelligence must be wrong—surely.

It's a lot to take in and I haven't even begun to deal with the part where she wanted me dead. Did she really want revenge bad enough to kill me? I'm innocent in all this, but to make my father pay by killing his child is sick.

I don't even register that Snake is still watching me because I am struggling to understand every word he just said. My father had an affair. I still can't believe it. How, why?

The bed dips and Snake says gently, "I'll fetch us a drink. I've got you, darlin', nobody will hurt you, I promise you that."

He drops a light kiss on the top of my head and leaves me to come to terms with a story that has destroyed my heart. Just thinking of my amazing, magnificent, adored father makes my blood run cold. How could he? Why - it doesn't make sense?

The more I think about it, the more the memories come back to haunt me. The spoiled dinners where mom always made excuses for him, blaming his work. The weekends he was missing, apparently out of state for work. The family gatherings where he never showed up due to work getting in the way. I was always proud of him. Always happy to hear the stories of his successes when he returned. Then I remember hearing the gentle sobs that echoed around a silent house at night. I thought mom missed him and could never understand why she struggled to accept his job. It was necessary, the endless hours away saving the world were the downside of justice.

It was why I wanted to be like him. To be as magnificent as he was, and now I can see it was all a pretense because he was probably with her.

Did mom know? My heart tells me she does, and that makes me wonder why she stayed. Then I think of my handsome, larger-than-life father, who when he was home was the beat of the heart that ran our lives. We orbited his soul because he was the most important person in our lives—though as it turns out, he was living two lives all the time.

My thoughts turn to the woman Snake described, and I wonder who she is? I rack my brains to think of the chain of command but can't think of any woman with the power to pull this off. The more I think, the harder my heart gets and I feel the bitterness tainting the shock as I come to terms with something that has altered everything. I know Snake is telling the truth, I saw it in his eyes. He was cool, calm and destructive and part of me is angry at him for telling me in the first place. The other part of me knows he had no choice and now it's up to me to deal with the information in the best way possible because one thing I do know, is that when we get out of here, the shit is going to hit the fan.

He enters the room and walks toward the bed and despite everything, my heart races when I see him. He's a warrior. A battle-hardened soldier with death in his eyes. He's so dangerous and wears it like a shield and just imagining that man inside me makes me wet already, which subsequently makes me feel disgusted with myself for desiring the man who has destroyed my life in seconds.

He hands me a whiskey and I throw back the contents in one go in an attempt to dull the pain, but I know it will take a lot more than this to make me feel normal again.

He looks concerned as he wraps a blanket around me and whispers, "Any questions, darlin'?"

I have lots of questions, so many questions, but none I want to deal with right now. Instead, I just reach for him and say huskily, "I don't want to talk about it. It's too much. Please, can we just do something to take my mind off it before I go slowly mad?"

He looks concerned and says in a worried voice, "You can't bottle it up, it will explode inside you and cause more damage."

"I know."

I look down and say in a broken voice, "It's just that I can't process the information right now. It's a lot to deal with and I have no way of making it all go away. Just for today, I want to pretend none of it is happening, will you help me?"

I look up at him and almost drown in those dangerous eyes as he growls low in his throat, "I will always make it go away, Bonnie. I meant what I said, you are coming home with me and we will face them together."

I still don't know what he means by that, and I shrug. "I'll be fine."

"With me."

"No, Snake, I have a life that is pretty shit right now, but if you think I'm going to turn my back on my problems and ride off into the sunset with you, then you're a fool."

I feel a little of the fire return as I push him away and stand. "I'm sorry, Snake, but this changes nothing. As soon as I can, I am heading back to work and I'm going to make them listen. I will tell them everything and whoever this bitch is, will pay. Then I'm going to make my father pay for not being the man I thought he was, and I'm going to tell my mom everything so she can make her own decision on whether she forgives him or not. I'm not sure if I ever can, but I need to sort this shit out and I will do that on my own."

Shrugging off the blanket, I reach for the cargo pants and t-shirt that have become the only items I possess right now and Snake says ominously, "What are you doing?"

"How the hell do I know?" I shout, in fact I scream at him as the tears blind my vision as I try to do anything to regain some control of my life.

It doesn't take me long to dress and I stand and look at him with determination. "Take me home."

"No, darlin'."

He runs his fingers through his hair wearily and says almost kindly, "I told you, we wait it out."

"Now!"

I am screaming but I don't care. This is so frustrating I want to deal with things, get some answers and make the bastards pay.

He stands and heads my way and I hold up my hand. "Stay away from me."

I don't want to see the hurt in his eyes knowing I'm the one responsible, but I'm losing my mind right now and as he advances, I back away angrily, "I said…"

Before the sentence even finishes, he grabs me hard and pulls me in so tight, I struggle to breathe. As those strong arms wrap around me, I stiffen and then out of nowhere, it comes. The emotion surges out like a raging rapid and I sob deeply into his chest as my world comes crashing down and he catches me as I fall. The tears have no ending and I have no answers. My life is out of my control and I have lost everything

I ever held dear. Nothing is as it seemed, and the only person here is the man who has turned me inside out in every way possible and broke me into shards of mistrust and regret. Regret for ever believing that all is good in the world and that I can make a difference because it's obvious I was used. I never earned my job, I was gifted it in exchange for my happiness because if my father had left, it would have destroyed us all.

CHAPTER 20

SNAKE

Bonnie is broken and sobs in my arms for what feels like hours. I will never let her go, not until she is able to make a rational decision. I wasn't lying when I said she was coming home with me because I will keep her here forever if I have to until she agrees to be by my side. I'm not letting her go and that may be the most selfish thing I have ever done, but just the thought of her not by my side is causing me to well and truly lose my shit.

By the time she calms down a few hours have passed and as she sleeps in my arms, I breathe a deep sigh of relief.

Now it's time to build her up and sort this shit out, so I edge away and wrap her up in the covers and leave her to sleep while I shower and try to form a plan.

I head outside as soon as I'm dressed and think about what happens next. I wasn't kidding when I said she had no job to return to, she's a target and would probably never make it past the door. I'm not sure she's ready to deal with that right now, so I grab my phone and make a call to see where we're at.

"Good to hear from you." Ryder's harsh tones settle me as a little piece of home sounds in my ear.

"You too, what's happening?"

"Still waiting on intel, Brewer's working fast but they won't move in until it's watertight. Why, are you sick of babysitting already?"

"I never said that."

Ryder laughs softly.

"Then why are you calling?"

"I need to know how long I've got."

"For...?"

"To persuade her I'm Prince fucking Charming, of course."

Ryder laughs loudly. *"Then it's been nice knowing you."*

Despite myself, I laugh. "Yeah, well, watch and learn."

"How is she?" Ryder sounds concerned and I sigh.

"Broken, usual shit."

There's a short silence and then he says with interest. *"So, what's your plan when you get the all clear?"*

"We're coming home."

"We?"

"Yes, we. You see, Ryder, Bonnie is going to be my old lady whether she knows it or not."

"I thought as much."

"You thought shit."

He laughs again. *"I knew the moment you laid eyes on that young lady. I've known you long enough to know you changed in a split second. I'm happy for you man, but send Bonnie my sympathies."*

"Fuck you, Ryder."

"Not today, I've got better things to do."

"Like exercising your hand, no doubt."

"Why would I when I have someone to do it for me?"

He laughs and then says darkly, *"Prepare her first, she is a Fed after all and we don't need that shit here."*

"Correction, Ryder, she *was* a Fed."

I cut the call and grin. Yes, Bonnie may think she's going back, but I have another plan in mind and it concerns her being under me and by my side 24/7.

It must be two hours later she emerges, blinking into the sunshine. Her hair is messed up and her eyes red from crying. To anyone else she looks like shit, to me she looks like everything I ever wanted.

I pat the seat next to me and smile. "Hey, baby, are you hungry?"

She half smiles and heads across and looks at me almost shyly. "Thanks, I am quite hungry. Extreme grief apparently does that to me."

She laughs to take the edge off her words and I look at her with concern.

"Do you wanna talk about it?"

"Perhaps, but not until I've eaten something."

Grabbing the sandwich I made for her, I hand it over and she accepts it gratefully "It's just ham and cheese, we should head into town and grab some more supplies."

"Town." Her eyes are wide as she takes a bite of the sandwich and I am struggling to tear my eyes from her mouth working the sub.

"Yeah, not far from here. I say town, it's more like one store but it stocks everything we need."

"Maybe I can grab a few things. I could pay you back when I get my stuff."

"No need, darlin', I can pay for anything you need."

She tucks her legs under her and looks at me thoughtfully. "So, tell me, what's it like being a Reaper?"

"The best." I smile and my heart settles when I think about my family. "It's filled with my best friends who are more like family now. We laugh, argue and fight and yet would lay down our life for every last fucker in there."

"Are they all ex-military?"

"No, not all, most though."

"How do they come to patch up?"

"They are invited."

I laugh softly. "You know, darlin', I can see now why you're a Fed, you sure ask a lot of questions."

"Am I?"

"What?"

"A Fed. I mean, you told me I had no job to go back to and I'm wondering what makes you think that? I mean, surely when this is over the job remains, they will know I was set up and I can carry on."

I've been expecting this question and say gently, "It's true, the job *is* still there but until this is settled you will never make it through that door."

Her eyes hold panic and I sigh. "Listen, I'm guessing the person who sent you there is sifting through the bodies as we speak, looking for evidence. It could take weeks to identify them all so she will be leaving nothing to chance until she has proof. She will be watching and has probably spun a tale that you're a rogue agent. Told the others to watch out for you and laid the blame for what happened squarely at your door."

"But…"

She blinks in disbelief and I shrug. "Self-preservation kicks in and she's doing what she must. If you're still out there, you will raise questions she doesn't want answered. She doesn't know about the other agent and doesn't know what you discovered. I'm guessing your name is dirt right now, and she's the one dishing it out. You would be arrested on sight and thrown in jail, pending an investigation. The evidence would point in your direction as a corrupt agent and you would be sent to prison, probably for life, if you make it to trial, that is."

"Who the fuck is this woman, surely, she wouldn't get away with that, it doesn't make sense?"

"It makes perfect sense because a scared criminal is a dangerous one. Fear makes us do things that no rational mind would ever think about. This woman will be covering her tracks and doing everything possible to shift the blame."

Bonnie slumps back against the seat and says quietly, "I guess, I just want to know one thing though."

"What?"

"Her name."

"Fiona Davenport."

Bonnie's eyes widen and the blood drains from her face. "Director Davenport."

I nod. "The same."

"But…"

"Now you can see how serious this is."

"But why is she concerned about me? I mean, that woman is second to God, she has it all."

"Not the one thing she wants."

"My father."

She shakes her head in disbelief and I sigh. "It's not just her private life that's turning to shit right now, it's her professional one too. She has many skeletons heading out of the closet like return of the zombies and she's desperate. The Knights of Hades were just one of the organizations in her pocket and the trouble with bargaining with criminals is you are never safe. She is being blackmailed in all directions and struggling to hold on. The secret service was drafted in to investigate those operations, and it's not just the Knights who were under the spotlight. That woman has so many lies unraveling I doubt she'll last the month, so you see we can't be the ones responsible for blowing it up before the timer runs out. Everything needs to be in place before the bomb goes off, otherwise there will be repercussions both of us sure don't need right now, so for everyone's benefit, we need to sit tight and wait it out."

My words have found their mark and her shoulders slump in defeat. "You win."

"I always do, darlin', get used to it."

She shakes her head and bites back. "You're a cocky son of a bitch, aren't you?"

"Guilty as charged."

For a moment we sit in silence as the situation settles around us and she looks to be deep in thought.

After a while, she sighs and stands, saying, "I'll head inside and change. A ride into town could be just what I need right now."

As I watch her leave, I wonder what's running through her mind because if I know the signs, I'd say she's plotting something and the last thing I want is to make her bad day a whole lot worse.

CHAPTER 21

BONNIE

I am numb. It's almost information overload, and I need time to organize my thoughts. Snake is right about one thing though, we need to sit tight because even I know this operation is way more important than me, Snake, or my father.

Thinking of my father hurts so much. I still can't get my head around his betrayal. He certainly moves in high places though, and my thoughts turn to the Director who wants him so badly she would kill. It doesn't sound as if she's thinking rationally, and I wonder about the woman who appears to have so much to the outside world but is living on a knife edge.

Maybe it was the secrecy, the forbidden element that attracted my father's interest. I've always known he's a handsome man. Mom's friends always looked at him a certain way, and I remember many guarded phone calls as he gave me a ride to class, or sleepovers. Were there other women? It wouldn't surprise me if there was, but why did mom put up with it? I feel so let down, more because I idolized a man who wasn't worth it. I wanted to be just like him and now I want to be everything he isn't. My life has flipped after one conversation and with a man I should be thinking of every way to escape from.

Thinking of Snake makes me shiver with excitement for a whole different reason. He is so dominant, and it surprises me that I like it—a lot. He tells rather than asks and demonstrates rather than describes, and I love that about him. It doesn't come without its problems though, and I will absolutely never let a man tell me what I can or can't do. But I can play the game and as I sift through the clothes that some misguided woman packed for me, I decide to push my trauma aside and let some light relief enter my world for a while because my head physically hurts when I think about the shit I'm in right now.

I need a distraction and that man is going to provide it for me, so I choose the outfit carefully and then step back and laugh at my reflection. Perfect.

Smoothing down the extremely short leather skirt, I appraise my reflection critically. The minuscule top she packed does little to contain my breasts and the skirt would show every part of me to anyone in front of me when I sit down. Grabbing a brush, I attack my wild hair until it hangs long down my back and grabbing the make-up she also packed, I outline my eyes in black and paint my lips as red as my hair. Then I climb onto the obscenely high heels and prepare to give that bastard a taste of what he thinks he wants.

Heading outside, I see him studying his phone and as he looks up, I struggle to keep the smile off my face. He looks so shocked it's the sweetest revenge as he drops his phone and mouth at the same time.

Standing before him, I say blankly, "I'm ready."

"For what?"

He can't stop staring at me with a mixture of horror and desire, and I cock my hip and pout suggestively. "Town. I thought we were going shopping."

"Not dressed like that, you're not."

"Why not, isn't this what you're used to?"

He appears speechless and I'm loving every second of it as he just looks and then shakes his head.

"The combats are fine."

"I'm bored with them; they could use a wash. Maybe there's a laundromat in town."

"Fuck me, Bonnie, go and change, that's an order."

"Make up your mind, fuck you, or change, it's your choice."

I start to giggle as he runs his fingers through his hair looking so conflicted, I wish I could capture the moment on video.

Then he says gruffly, "If you dress like a whore, I'll treat you like one."

"Go on then, what would you do if a whore was standing here now?"

I am so up for this game because just seeing him lose control like this is the best revenge ever and then I see the dark glint in his eye that is turning me on so much, as he barks, "Come here."

I wander across as sexily as these fucking heels will allow and as I reach him, he pulls me across his knee and my heart sinks. Not again.

I feel him running his hand under my skirt and he pinches my ass hard. Lowering his lips to my ear, he whispers, "First, I like to spank them a little and warm them up. Then I like to watch them suck my cock on their knees where they belong."

He runs his fingers through my hair and grabs a handful and pulls my head back roughly.

"Then I fuck their smart mouth until they gag and pull them up to ride my cock until I say stop. Then, only when I've had my fun, are they free to leave."

"Not much in it for them, is there?"

I shake my head in apparent disgust and he shrugs. "That's why they're whores, it's no fairy story."

Pushing up, I straddle his lap and lean down and whisper, "You're a liar."

"Is that so?"

His grin tells me I'm right and I reach down and cup his balls hard. "I'm guessing you try everything possible to make it memorable because after all, you wouldn't want them running around that place you call home saying how shit you are in the sack."

He laughs out loud and I grin impishly. "So, what do you like, Snake? Do you like a woman to dress like she's gagging for it, or do you respect a woman's choice to dress how she damn well likes?"

He pulls my head down toward his lips and whispers, "I like them hot, willing and able. I like a woman with sass and fire running through her veins. I like a woman with a quick wit and I like her to be so god damned sexy, my balls physically ache every time I look at her. The first woman who ticked all those boxes was you, Bonnie, so now you see why I insist you stay."

He has taken away any smart retort I had prepared and as the tears spring to my eyes, I am speechless. As moments go, this one is unexpected because he has revealed a side to him I never saw before. He wasn't joking. He is serious and my breath hitches as I see the hunger in his eyes for *me* and yet how can I give him what he wants? I'm not a biker's girl, I'm a cop and I will fight for that right. But Snake is so unexpected, so delicious and so dark, I'm blinded by my overwhelming need for him in my life.

He leans forward and captures my lips and I taste something special. Any fight I had inside me can be dealt with later because it's important to savor this moment—with him. He is the breath in my lungs and the life in my veins right now and as I kiss him back, I feel as if I am floating on a lust driven cloud outlined with love.

Is it possible to fall in love with someone so quickly, or is it just lust blinding me to the imperfections that would drive a wedge between us? I need time to figure that out, so I kiss him back with an impatience to learn what this is between us.

He holds my head hard and kisses me so softly—as if he really loves me and is treating me like a princess. It's such a powerful gift to possess because it makes me want to do anything for him.

The kiss deepens, and he groans as I shift with impatience on his lap and as he hooks up my skirt so I grind against his cock, I am desperate to feel it inside me. He lifts off my top and takes one of my breasts in his mouth and sucks hard, making me squirm with desire on his lap. My fingers move to unfasten his jeans and he shifts so I can pull them down a little, allowing his cock to spring free.

Carefully, he lifts my hips and lowers me down until I feel him slide in, slowly, carefully and filling me to the hilt. His cock jerks inside me and causes the juices to welcome him in. As he moves slowly, I capture a moan in the back of my throat because he makes me feel so desirable, so sexy and so screwed because how can I turn my back on this kind of loving with such a man? No one has ever come close to him before now and every minute we spend together is a moment to treasure because it's as if we're in our own world right now, where real life can't inflict the usual damage it usually aims at me.

I ride him in the open air as if I'm taking a gentle ride through the mountains. It's not frantic, hot or dirty, it's calm, slow and sexy. Bonnie and Snake are making love right now, so leave a message and they'll get back to you because nothing can interrupt this moment of pleasure.

As the birds call their encouragement and the wind whips around us with interest, I come so hard it feels as if my whole body shatters to the ground below. Snake has ruined me for any other man because I have never felt as complete as I do right now, coming soon after everything I held close has been wrenched from me in one cruel conversation.

This is my new beginning, and yet am I ready for that? Feeling him shoot his seed so hard inside me, I know my answer as he roars like the king of the jungle. Yes, fate has turned over her winning card because I couldn't give him up now if I tried.

CHAPTER 22

SNAKE

When Bonnie heads toward me a second time, I nod my appreciation.

"That's better."

"Why, didn't you like it?"

She is once again dressed in the combats and loose-fitting t-shirt and I growl, "I don't want any other man looking at my property."

"Your property, what are you, some kind of misogynist asshole now?"

"You guessed it."

I grin as she rolls her eyes. "We need to work on that."

"You can work on me anytime you like, darlin', I'll not apologize for who I am."

Flicking her hair back, she slides behind me on the bike and I'm loving every second of it. Pulling down the helmet over her gorgeous face, she says roughly, "Just drive before I lay you out cold."

Laughing, I turn on the engine and relish the hum of the engine as my pride and joy bursts into life and right now I have everything I want in life here on this bike.

DIRTY HERO

As we head into town, I wonder how long this will last. Life has a habit of getting in the way sometimes, and I'm dreading the day Ryder calls and tells us to head back. Will she come, it's 50/50 right now because I know she will have scores to settle and want to pay her family a visit? I'm happy to go with her because letting her out of my sight for one minute isn't an option right now because until I know she's one hundred percent safe, she's going nowhere without me.

We head to the store and I make sure to pay attention. I feel pretty safe here and Elias would have called if anyone was sniffing around, but I'm too battle worn to take anything for granted, so I recon the area before stopping and parking up outside the only store in town.

We head inside and I let Bonnie wander the aisles as I keep a look out by the door and I love watching her more than anything right now. She appears so small in the oversized clothes, but looks like a goddess as her red hair tumbles down her back and her ass wiggles as she moves. I love her like this the most. The whore's clothes did nothing for me, if I'm honest, it's not her - not Bonnie. She is better than that and looks best when she's relaxed and at ease with herself, and if that's when she's dressed like a man, so be it.

I notice a few guys giving her the eye, which are quickly lowered when I glare at them. I know I frighten people. Hell, I've made a career out of it but not her. I don't want to scare her away, yet sometimes I can't help the bastard in me taking over.

She heads toward the counter and places her basket on the side, and the assistant looks her over dismissively. As she rings up the groceries, I watch the woman closely because one word said out of turn will cause my hackles to rise.

In a bored voice, she says in a southern drawl, "$49.97." Bonnie looks round and I hold out my card. "Here you go, darlin'."

The woman looks at Bonnie as if she's dirt, and Bonnie looks awkward because I'm guessing she hates having to ask me to pay for this. She's an independent woman and would pay her way, but that's not an option right now, so I grab the receipt and stare the woman down.

"Your customer service skills suck, darlin'. Next time remember the customer is king and never, I repeat, never look at my woman like that again."

The woman steps back a little and looks fearful, and Bonnie grabs my arm and pulls me away.

"For fuck's sake, Snake, do you want to draw attention to us? You know, for someone who is a self-styled fucking warrior, you sure are a dumbass sometimes."

We exit the shop and I snarl, "What did you just call me?"

I love the way all the blood drains from her face as she remembers what happened the last time she called me by that name and she checks herself and says, "I'm sorry, I didn't mean to be rude but, well..."

"You're learning."

I grin as she rolls her eyes. "But you are and you know it."

Slapping her on her ass, she yelps as I head toward the bike. "Yeah, but it takes one to know one."

"Did you really just call me a dumbass?"

She faces me with her hands on her hips and I nod. "If the cap fits."

She walks toward me slowly and with menace in her eyes and whispers, "Then you'll pay for that in the usual manner."

"Is that so." Laughing, I store the bags on my bike and before I know it, I'm flat on my back in the dust as she sits astride my neck, her fingers cupped around my balls. "Just so you know, soldier, I'm not one to let a smart remark go unpunished."

Rolling her over and gripping her hands real tight, I whisper, "Then I'll accept my punishment gladly, but just so you know, darlin', you've got to catch me first and if you ever get that far, you had better be prepared for the consequences."

I lift her effortlessly to her feet and thrust the helmet at her.

"Come on, I've worked up quite an appetite,"

I hear her giggle escape that she is trying to contain and I love the way she makes me feel. I still can't believe how perfect she is for me and I'm impatient to make it legal and above board so Bonnie knows this is not a game and for life because I only want one woman in mine and she's the one holding on tight as we head back to the cabin.

CHAPTER 23

BONNIE

The next few days are probably the best in my life, so far, anyway. Snake is the perfect companion in every way. Attentive, funny, charming even and so god damned sexy my body can't believe its luck. Most of the time we're exploring each other, but occasionally we put each other down and head out to explore this amazing mountain and all it has to offer. It's as if we have no cares, no worries, and as the days turn into weeks, I almost forget why we're here at all.

I'm not sure at what point I fell in love with him, but he has somehow wrapped himself around my heart like a protective layer. I feel as if nothing can hurt me all the time I'm with him because he makes me feels so loved. He spends hours teaching me how to survive, to fight and to cope with just about anything life throws at me and I'm grateful for that because the more time that passes brings me closer to the realization there is still a big black cloud on my horizon that threatens to tear down everything I've built.

The call comes when we least expect it and after yet another luxurious shower to wash away probably two hours of passion with Snake, I emerge to find him deep in conversation outside. He is holding his phone to his ear looking pissed and my heart freezes as I sense things are about to change.

His eyes meet mine and he looks worried, which isn't like him and my breath hitches as I feel uncomfortable about what's coming next.

"We'll be there."

He cuts the call and sighs heavily, opening his arms and nodding for me to head to his side.

I don't even think because for some reason I only want to be there anyway and as his strong arms close around me, I am fearful to hear his next sentence.

"It's done, baby, we are needed back home."

"What's done?"

I swear my heart is jumping all over the place and he sighs.

"While we've been enjoying ourselves, the authorities have also been busy. The operation has moved on and the Director is facing charges."

I pull back and look at him in shock. "You're kidding me."

"It's all over the news. She's been arrested and is currently awaiting trial for every fucking reason they can throw at her. All her lies are unraveling and you must return for a debrief."

I start to shake because suddenly I'm scared. My own crimes are coming back with a vengeance right now, and I can't help the tears that spring forward as I remember that I killed a man.

Snake looks wretched which makes me worry even more and sighing he drops to his knees and presses his face against my stomach and groans. "I fucking hate this, but know I'm with you every step of the way. First, we head home, then we listen. Ryder has assured me he's cleared it with your department, but you will have to make a statement."

"What will I say?"

My mind is all over the place right now and Snake pulls me down beside him and slings his arm around my shoulders and growls, "The truth. You tell them everything that happened and leave nothing out. You see, darlin', you've done nothing wrong and have nothing to fear. Blaze had it coming, and there is no need to dodge the issue. It was self-defense and you have a bunch of bastards as witnesses. It's doubtful your boss will even ask, but I'm guessing he needs to tie up any loose ends so there's no comeback on any of you, then there's your family."

"What about them?" My gut wrenches in pain as I think about facing them. So much has happened, I'm not sure I can look at them in the same way again. The fact they thought I was dead was a blessing in disguise because it's given me time to think and now I'm going to have to face them with the knowledge of what my father has done, probably for my entire life.

"Do they know I'm alive?"

My voice comes out in a whisper but is loud inside my head as I scream with fear. "Yes."

"Ok." I nod slowly, still confused as to what the hell is happening right now, and Snake sighs.

"Tell me one thing."

"What?"

"If they ask you to return to work, what will you do?"

Suddenly, it's out there, hanging in the surrounding air. The moment of decision because when we leave this place, it will change everything.

Picturing my old life, my amazing, exciting, noble life that I was so proud of, seems so insignificant right now at the realization that Snake cannot be part of it. I'm not stupid, I know our worlds don't mix and even if we tried, circumstances would tear us apart. I have lots of decisions to make and I doubt many of them are in my control, but my heart is ripping apart in two ways and the pain is almost unbearable.

Reaching out, I lace my fingers with his and stare deep into his troubled eyes and my own tears spill as I struggle to form words. "I don't want to lose you, but in keeping you I lose myself."

He nods as if he understands exactly what I'm saying and squeezes my hand back as he sighs. "It's your decision to make, but if you come home with me, you know I will it make it my life's work to make you happy. The job has to go because of how we live—what we do. I know I'm asking a lot of you, Bonnie. You have a lot to deal with and yet the only thing I care about is that you are by my side. We can work out the details later, but that is the most important thing, the rest are just details.

He lifts his hand and strokes my face gently and his eyes glitter like two stars in the blackest sky. "I love you, Bonnie Anderson. You may irritate the shit out of me, you're impulsive, and your backchat tests my patience more than anyone I've ever met. You don't follow instruction and to a man used to complete submission, you write your own agenda. You're sexy, smart and the perfect girl for me and I have never met anyone who matches me so perfectly. From the moment I learned there was love in this world, I started searching for you. I found you in a dark place and I carried you out of danger. I will always be the devil riding shotgun on your shoulder because nobody messes with him. You are the best part of me and I am the worst part of you, opposites that attract but need each other to survive. Don't even think about telling me I'm wrong because we both know I'm always right."

He laughs softly and dips his head to capture my lips and pulling back, whispers, "I love you enough to let you go if that is your choice. I want what's best for you, Bonnie, and if you decide that isn't me, I will walk away but leave my heart in your capable hands, so if you ever feel the need to give it back, I will be waiting."

It's too much, *he's* too much because I already know I couldn't give him up if I tried. I may think it's for the best to head home and carry on as before, make the world a better place legally and above board, but I've changed. So, I shake my head and say with determination,

"You think it's that easy? You think I'm giving up on us before we've even started. Well, think again, soldier, because somebody needs to keep you in line. You may think you're the big badassed biker who can power through life on a wing and a prayer. You need me just as much as I need you, and we will work something out that suits us both. I'm kind of greedy like that because I want it all and it's up to us to work as a team to make sure I get it."

He doesn't even wait for the last word to leave my lips before his mouth is on mine, crushing me with emotion. His tongue captures mine and reminds me why I'm going nowhere but with him and as he presses me down into the dirt, it becomes the most urgent thing in the world to feel him inside me right now.

Like two frenzied wild animals, we edge out of our clothes and as my legs wrap around his waist, he drives in deep. Feeling Snake inside me is like returning home after a hard day at the office. It's the place I physically ache to be and the one that drives every problem, every decision needed away. The world makes sense when we're together and nothing else matters. He came into my life in the most destructive of ways, but when storms hit, they are a force of nature that can alter everything. My life is different now and I am not alone anymore. Snake and Bonnie made it through and I really believe that because when I head home to face my demons, it's with a devil by my side.

How can I possibly fail?

CHAPTER 24

SNAKE

She may have reassured me, but I'm still antsy as hell. The moment we left the cabin, my head started throwing every reason why this isn't gonna work at me. She held on tight for the entire journey and I know she feels it too. We may have come to some kind of decision back there, but making it work is a whole different ballgame.

The first hurdle to jump is taking her home, and I wonder what she'll think of that. It's nowhere near as fucked up as the Hades clubhouse, but it's not far off. Fifty men live at the Rubicon and they all need a warm body to hide inside when the blood is washed from their hands after a hard day in the field. Whores, old ladies and those in between, make up a community that many wouldn't believe if they saw it right before their eyes. Can Bonnie deal with life at The Rubicon, 'the point of no return' because our clubhouse was named that way for a very good reason.

The Twisted Reaper MC is a decision made because when we come calling, it's dishing out the punishment earned. Yes, we all face our point of no return at some time in life and this is mine and Bonnie's. The moment she steps inside the Rubicon, things change for us both forever. If she chooses to step outside, I know she will take the best part of me with her and I wasn't kidding about that.

So, as I turn off the highway and head down the familiar street to the dusty track that disguises hell, my heart beats faster than it ever has before because what happens next will change the course of my life forever.

Her decision comes wrapped up in the gravest consequences, and I'm not sure I'm ready for what they will be.

The sight of the sunlight reflecting off the metal of a bunch of Harleys all lined up outside a steel-clad building makes my heart swell. I'm home.

This place will always be home to me because this is where my family live.

The Reapers, blood brothers who I trust with my life and it's important that Bonnie understands that. It's more important that these bastards understand what she is to me too, because if one of them so much as looks at her in the wrong way, I am liable to lose my shit.

As I pull up, I'm surprised to see Ryder waiting. Unusual and it makes my heart beat a little faster as he sits on the step watching us approach through his enigmatic eyes.

He is alone, which again surprises me because most of the whores inside won't leave him alone for one second which I know drives him insane most of the time. Ryder King is bastard number one and gives nothing away. They all try to be his old lady, but he has no interest in forming any longstanding connections. If he thinks one of them is getting ideas, he moves onto the next. It frustrates the hell out of them and drove one ambitious lady to get pregnant in the hope he would make her his old lady. When she gave birth to his daughter, she became the most important thing in his life and her mother's job was to care for his daughter and stay the fuck away from him. Ryder carried on doing what he always did, and Eva had a kid to care for instead. Cassie is the most adorable angel that we all watch over, and I pity whoever tries to get in the way of that.

Bonnie is quiet beside me as we head toward him, and I grab her hand and twist our fingers together to give her comfort and show Ryder what he's dealing with.

His eyes glitter as we approach, and I see the slight smirk on his face as he nods.

"Good to see you, Snake."

Standing, he heads down the steps and I feel Bonnie shake a little beside me as he looks her in the eye and smiles, "I'm sorry, darlin'."

She tenses immediately and he grins. "It looks as if you've had a hard time and I am sorry for your situation."

"Fuck you, Ryder."

I roll my eyes and Bonnie shifts a little closer as Ryder laughs. "Welcome, Bonnie, you must have many questions, but before we go inside, I want to reassure you."

His voice sounds almost kind as he smiles softly. "You are not in the frame for killing Blaze."

"How?" Her voice sounds weak with relief and yet there's an edge to it that tells me she's still unsure about the whole situation and he shrugs. "Turns out there was an explosion at The Knights of Hades' clubhouse. A faulty gas tank, would you believe. There wasn't much left once the bodies were counted, and it's gone down as a terrible accident. Shocking really when you come to think of it, they really should have kept up to date with their certificates. Such a waste."

His eyes find mine and I nod, knowing that this is one demon Bonnie won't have to face and I'm grateful for that. I always knew it would be the case, but she needed to hear it before we deal with the rest.

She nods, and I can tell she's intimidated by him. We all are, but I know him more than most to know it's all a front. Ryder King is the kindest, most loyal and patriotic man to walk this earth and he will always have our backs. It's why he's so good at what he does because his actions are driven by honor and nobody messes with that.

He stands aside and says darkly, "It's a full house in there and you may want to settle Bonnie in first before she sees what a bastard she's come home with."

"Home." Her voice shakes a little and Ryder looks surprised and then laughs softly, "Interesting."

"It's Bonnie's choice." I shrug and Ryder looks at me with a hard expression because he knows I'm not so casual inwards as I am letting on.

Bonnie nods. "I'm not sure what's happening, but I expect I'll be leaving soon. Snake said something about a debrief with my department and then there's my family…"

She looks worried and Ryder nods. "Of course. It's all arranged. Settle in here first, then tomorrow you have a meeting back at the department. Your family expects you after that and it's your decision where you go from here. You need all the facts first, which is why Snake brought you here. Brewer will fill you in but not before you eat."

As we follow him inside, I wonder what the next 24 hours will bring. Destiny or destruction, hers or mine, I'm not sure which one has my name written on it, but I will do my darndest to persuade her our future's here—together.

CHAPTER 25

BONNIE

I'm already terrified and we haven't even got inside. Ryder King scares the shit out of me because I don't think I've ever met such an enigma in my life. Danger swirls around him like a warning not to touch, and just one look from him causes my soul to cower in fear. If the devil had a body, it's living inside the one who is guiding us into a place I almost want to close my eyes on and imagine I'm somewhere else.

As soon as we head through a large wooden door, I see we're in a hallway that appears to go on for miles. Snake calls it a compound, and it certainly feels that way as I notice the cameras set up watching every move we make. The fact Ryder was waiting tells me he saw us coming, and I wonder about this place. It's like a prison and I almost expect metal gates to close behind me and lock automatically because it certainly feels like there's no escape.

Ryder and Snake talk in low even sentences, but I hear nothing. I'm too worried to listen and feel so intimidated I'm struggling to breathe.

We reach a door about halfway down and I blink as we head

into an office. It must be Ryder's because he heads around a large desk and nods toward two chairs set up in front of it.

Snake smiles reassuringly, but my insides are in knots as I sit shivering in the seat as if I'm waiting for a life sentence.

Ryder lifts his phone and barks, "Snakes' here, bring us some beers and coffee for the lady. Oh, and send Brewer in."

He cuts the call and looks thoughtful. "Are you hungry, I can arrange food?"

I shake my head because food is the furthest thing from my mind right now and Snake says quickly, "We'll grab something in the cafeteria after."

"You sure that's a good idea?"

Ryder fixes him with a look that makes me even more uncomfortable and Snake says tersely, "Bonnie's fine, she can handle the Rubicon."

Ryder leans back and turns his attention to me, and I feel as if he's carrying out some kind of assessment. "It's not as bad as it looks, darlin' and any trouble you have Snake to turn to and if the troubles from him, come to me."

Snake swears and the words he uses are new even for me and Ryder laughs, which surprises me again. They're like two bickering brothers, one existing just to wind the other up and seeing their obvious love for one another settles my heart—a little.

We all look up as the door opens and I see a familiar face heading inside, although this time he is dressed as I would expect.

He grins wickedly when he sees me and winks before taking the seat beside Ryder and saying kindly, "We meet again under much happier circumstances."

Holding out his hand, he says, "Brewer, priest impersonator and life saver when I'm not taking them."

I feel so grateful to him, I can't even form the right kind of words to describe how much his actions mean to me and all I can do is say emotionally, "Thank you for saving my life."

He nods, but I can see he feels the emotion too and just nods before looking across at Snake and grinning. "No, darlin', it's us who should be thanking you. It's been paradise around here without your man there bugging the shit out of us. Shame a good thing had to end."

Snake smirks as I say sharply, "My man, what the fuck, does everyone know something I don't?"

They all laugh and Snake reaches across and grabs my hand before saying smugly, "Fight it all you want, darlin', none of us believe for one second that you're going anywhere."

The two other men shake their heads and despite the fact I want to tear him a new set, we share a look that would cause that gas explosion in the Hades' clubhouse. Yes, we all know what's written in the stars and I'm not about to deny something that is the best thing that's ever happened to me.

Once again, the door opens and I just stare in stunned awe at the beautiful woman heading inside, balancing a tray. She looks at Ryder first and I see a deep yearning for approval in her eyes but he just says tersely, "Thanks, darlin', leave it on the desk."

Her eyes swing to me and I see the curiosity burning in them and something about this woman makes me feel a little sad. I don't think I've ever seen such a beautiful woman dressed liked a whore. Her short skirt barely covers her ass and her long dark wavy hair almost touches her waist. Those dark brown eyes are so deep I am lost in them and her face would be any artist's life's desire to paint. However, the guys don't appear to notice her and just carry on ribbing each other, and as she glances my way, I offer her a small smile of thanks. I get nothing back though because if anything she looks pissed to see me and I wonder about the women in this place.

Before she goes, she hovers on the edge of the group as if

she wants something and Ryder just says darkly, "That's all, Kitty."

She nods and turns to leave, and for some reason it makes me consider my desire to stay. Is this how they treat the women in this place? As if they don't matter and are just there to serve their needs in every way.

Ryder's hard voice drags my attention back to the job in hand and he says evenly, "There's a meeting set up tomorrow with your boss, Bonnie. The story is that the undercover operative rescued you from Blaze and took you to hide out at a safe house until the coast was clear. He returned to his department for a full de-brief but warned you to stay hidden until the matter was resolved. He has told them things got out of hand that night and Blaze was out of his head on alcohol and you weren't safe. The intelligence he fed back caused the Director to panic and as soon as questions started being asked, she dug herself more into the hole than out of it. Her conversations were recorded and cover was blown and she was arrested the next day for questioning. Every dirty contact she has in her little black book has been hauled in, and none of them seem inclined to protect her ass. You're in the clear and nobody knows what really went down that night, so if you wanted you could return to work and carry on as before."

He smiles, but it's laced with questions as he looks at Snake and I feel the tension in the room. They are all waiting for me to speak and I know that my decision has many consequences and I'm just not ready to face them.

Reaching across, I take Snake's hand and don't miss the smirk on Ryder's face but I don't care about that. All I care about is reassuring him that I may be undecided but my heart lies with him.

I brave a look and see the storm in his eyes mixed with a hint of fear that I hate seeing because I don't want to be the person responsible for bringing this man down, so I say carefully, "Thank you, that's a load off my mind. I am so grateful."

Brewer smiles. "You'll be fine, darlin', whatever you decide you'll be ok."

I return his smile but I'm not so sure because will I be—ok that is, because if I walk away from Snake, I'll be fine from ok but if I stay, do I lose myself in the process?

CHAPTER 26

SNAKE

Despite the fact I love being home, I'm hating every minute of this. There are so many questions up in the air waiting to connect with the right answer, and I'm fearful that I won't like what I hear. Bonnie is quiet, which isn't like her and I tell she's conflicted. Hell, I would be too, so I am trying hard to keep my shit together and trust in the lady who has stormed into my heart and let off a grenade.

We finish up and I take her hand and leave the men behind and as soon as we're on our own, Bonnie looks up at me through tortured eyes. "So, this is it, my Rubicon."

"I guess it is."

We walk hand in hand down the corridor and I direct her to the cafeteria where we could sure use some food right now. This place may be my home but I'm guessing it seems a pretty scary place for her at this moment and I'm annoyed about that because actually this is the safest place in the whole of the country because we're here—the Reapers. Nobody messes with us, not even the authorities—hell, *especially* the authorities because we have so much dirt on them, they would be buried in a matter of seconds.

We reach the cafeteria and I say with a sigh, "Come on, darlin', we need to eat and just for the record, ignore every bastard inside this room because they will have only one thing on their mind when they lay their eyes on you and I'm liable to lose my shit inside of sixty seconds."

She rolls her eyes and pouts. "Honestly, Snake, you're such a caveman sometimes. I'm not your private property you know, you really should seek counseling for this problem you have."

She giggles as I toss her over my shoulder and slap her ass hard and growl, "Is that caveman enough for you? I told you, I'll not apologize for who I am."

Setting her down, I love the fact her arms wrap around me and she presses her cheek to my chest and says huskily, "I love you just the way you are."

"You love me." I can't stop the smug satisfaction creeping into my voice and she giggles. "Figure of speech, asshole."

"Keep telling yourself that darlin', we both know you adore every inch of me and you can't deny fact."

She pulls back and I love the sight of her eyes flashing as she prepares to deliver a sharp retort but before she can, I kick the door open distracting her attention and the noise greets us as we step into the large open space of a place filled with hungry Reapers and the women who live here.

The noise only increases when we step inside the room and for a while we're caught up in a barrage of taunts, greetings and interest, and I feel Bonnie's shock as she grips my hand tightly. I know it's a sight not many are keen to witness because all around us is more ink and muscle than is good for you. The guys are crude and alphaholes and the women are predatory and protective over their property. Luckily, I spy one woman who won't want to warn Bonnie off anytime soon and I drag her across to the table she's sitting at with Maverick, who looks up with interest. "Hey, Snake, good to see you."

His eyes turn to Bonnie and I glare, making him laugh and

an amused glint hit his eye. "This is Bonnie, make sure everyone knows she's with me."

I don't miss the surprise on Lexi's face as she looks at Bonnie with curiosity and then smiles as I knew she would.

"Hey, I'm pleased to meet you, sweetheart, come and sit with me. Thank God for someone normal to chat to."

Maverick shakes his head as Lexi bats her lashes at him and blows him a kiss. "Present company aside, that is, you know I love you, Mav."

He just rolls his eyes and I'm glad to see the relief on Bonnie's face as she takes the seat beside Lexi.

"I'll fetch us some food, you'll be ok with Lexi."

Bonnie nods and I feel her eyes follow me as I head over to the counter where Angel's on duty today, feeding the horde of bastard bikers.

As I approach, she looks at me with a huge smile. "Hey, baby, we missed you."

Angel is one of my favorite whores because she never seems to get down. Always happy to listen and doesn't get involved in any of the games most of them try. She's been with us around a year already and I know she's healing from a stunt her family pulled on her, which led her to run away and find herself in a whole heap of trouble. Luckily, we were at the end of that trouble and brought her here until she decides what to do next.

"So, tell me, who's the pretty lady on your arm?"

She starts shoveling food onto the plate and I say lightly, "Bonnie, ex-Fed and soon to be my old lady."

Angel's eyes widen in disbelief. "Wow, I never saw that one coming."

"Neither did I."

I grin and she nods, a huge smile on her face as she says softly, "I'm happy for you, Snake, you deserve someone nice."

"Don't we all."

For a moment her eyes cloud with pain and I think on the

reason she's here at all. The usual bastard boyfriend breaking her heart and is probably the reason why she likes living here—no commitment, no drama, just a warm body to curl up with of a night and no demands on anything she's not willing to give. Unlike the Knights of Hades, the Reapers are all about protection and would never force any woman to do anything they weren't wanting 100%.

She laughs softly as she hands me one plate and whispers, "Does she know any of this?"

"10/10 for observation, darlin', she soon will though."

Angels shakes her head. "Then she must be one strong woman to commit to taking you on. Maybe I should have a word—warn her of the consequences of that."

"I know you love me; you're probably just pissed it's not you in her place."

Handing me the second plate, she shakes her head. "Keep telling yourself that, biker, the only one who believes it is your over inflated ego."

I laugh as I turn away and catch sight of Bonnie across the room looking scared shitless but somehow at home in this hellish place. Luckily, there's only a handful of bikers here. It's mainly just the single bikers who eat here, the married ones preferring to dine with their families in their homes out the back of the compound. It will be interesting to show Bonnie around and see what she makes of it because I'm guessing she will be surprised because it's nothing like people think. We are a community, a family, and it's not just bikers who live here. It's their wives, kids and animals and that's what keeps us all from going slightly mad. A normal life existing in chaos, the perfect place for me and Bonnie to start our lives together.

CHAPTER 27

BONNIE

I'm not sure what to make of this place because it's so different from how I imagined. It's clean, orderly, and yet filled with so much menace I'm struggling to breathe. I didn't miss the slightly hostile looks thrown my way by some of the women as we walked into the room, probably because of the ones the men with them threw my way. It felt as if I was naked in a sea of sharks and they were sizing up their next meal and I was grateful for Snake's hand holding mine so tenderly as we ventured inside.

He is like walking protection, which I am glad about because of everyone here, he is the most menacing. He has a commanding air that follows him around, and I see the reverence in everyone's eyes as they look at him. They respect him, it's obvious and I feel strangely proud about that. It feels good holding his hand as we head inside and as soon as I laid my eyes on Lexi, I relaxed because she is like a breath of normality in an extremely abnormal situation.

She looks at me with curiosity rather than animosity, and the guy with her settles back and looks at me through the darkest hooded expression. He is slightly wild with longish hair that hits his shoulders and dark flashing eyes that give nothing away but a promise of so much darkness it's doubtful you would survive to see the light again.

Like all of them, this man is formed of more muscle than I have ever seen, and the ink that decorates his arms is stretched across him like a battle cry.

Lexi looks at him pointedly and he says gruffly, "I'll leave you to it, you up for poker later, Lexi?"

"Sure, if you're prepared to lose again."

She winks at me as he shakes his head, and I'm surprised to hear a low rumble of laughter leave his throat. "Yeah, well, we'll just have to see about that."

As he leaves, Lexi giggles beside me and whispers, "That man is the only one who can beat me at poker. His poker face is almost as good as mine."

I watch him leave and wonder about him. He seemed nice enough, but there was something about him that doesn't fit with his surroundings. It feels as if he's wearing the wrong identity and I can't put my finger on why.

Lexi leans in and whispers, "Don't be put off by these guys, Bonnie. They may look like tigers, but they're pussycats underneath. You're perfectly safe here, especially with the protection you've got walking beside you, I mean way to go honey, you scored the perfect ten with Snake."

My eyes find him across the room, chatting to a pretty blonde who seems nice enough and Lexi says, "That's Angel, one of the whores. Don't hold it against her though, she's nicer than most."

"I can't believe they call them whores, it's so degrading."

Lexi shakes her head. "No, the whores like it that way. Most of them are here on a temporary visa and don't want to be tied down. They're keen to eat the candy on offer but don't want the commitment being with one of the guys involves."

"What commitment?"

Thinking of my own situation, I'm keen to discover what that is and Lexi sighs. "They're hard to deal with because once a Reaper takes an old lady, they're here for life. Don't get me wrong, you wouldn't find a better life anywhere else because these guys treat their women well. They are loyal, kind and so sexy it's hard to think past the obvious sometimes, but it's not for everyone."

"Are you an old lady, Lexi?" It sounds ridiculous as I say it and she throws her head back and laughs. "God no, I'm no whore either, I'm probably the only exception to the rule though."

I look at her with curiosity and she smiles proudly. "I'm a Reaper, Bonnie. The only female one to my knowledge there has ever been. The guys are my brothers, and the thought of being with any of them would be like fucking my own family. Don't get me wrong, a few have tried, but I've set them straight and they don't try again."

She grins and I stare at her in total surprise because Lexi looks like unicorns and rainbows and every Disney princess you have ever seen. There's a softness to her, an innocence wrapped in fairy dust, as she gazes at me through large baby blue eyes that shine from a beautiful face. Her hair is golden and hangs in curls to her shoulders, and she looks as if she would snap if you handled her too harshly.

She laughs at the shock on my face and says sweetly, "When I came to live here it was to hide from my folks. I won't bore you with the details, but this life interested me. My brother Chase was with me and he started training almost immediately. It took me a few weeks longer to convince them to include me in that, but if you want something bad enough, then you don't stop until it's yours."

I laugh at the determination in her eyes and she laughs softly. "The guys hated training with me because they were afraid of breaking me. It taught me a lot because I soon learned skills I would never have imagined and by the time I was through the basics, I was hooked."

"So, what's your job now?" I can't believe a woman like Lexi would have been sent out to kill a roomful of men like the guys and she grins. "I work in a more subtle way. They send me in when the target is more refined and they need someone to look the part. It's fun most of the time, but I have my rules and they break them at their peril."

"What are your rules?"

"Definitely no touching. That would send me down a road I'm not about to set foot on. This place should be renamed the devil's temptation because god knows, it takes a strong woman to resist these bastards."

As I look around, I have to agree because the testosterone in this room is dominating the oxygen right now and Lexi says sweetly, "Most of the time I'm away on an operation. I'm back until the next one and just enjoying some down time for a while. I'm considering taking off though and traveling. I have a friend in Canada I'm keen to visit and may take an extended vacation."

"On your own?"

I am so impressed by Lexi and she nods. "Yeah, I had a particularly difficult mission last, that I'm trying to come to terms with, so I feel as if I need some distance for a while. This life is hard, Bonnie, but the rewards more than make up for it I'm undecided what to do next, so I thought I'd take some time out for *me* for once."

"I know that feeling."

Thinking about my own situation, I could use some time to make my decision and she looks sympathetic. "Listen, sweetie, don't be swayed by the big bad bastard, you do what's best for Bonnie. One thing I'll say about Snake is you would struggle to find a better man. Under all that cockiness and muscle, there's a soft heart just desperate to find his soul mate. The fact he's been away so long tells me he's found her, but you must feel exactly the same for it to work. If it does, you will never look back, and that's a promise because once you claim a Reaper's heart, you've won at life.

We watch as Snake heads back and I can't ignore the flutter in my stomach as he smiles at me across the room. Lexi laughs softly beside me and says, "I never thought I'd see the day."

"What?"

"When Snake fell in love."

Her words hit me hard.

"Love, I think you've got that wrong. He may like me, desire me even, but I doubt he loves me."

She laughs. "Listen, honey, I know that man and he has never looked at anyone the way he is looking at you now. Trust me, I know how to read people, it's why I'm good at what I do and if that man isn't head over heels in love with you, I'm losing my touch."

As Snake joins us, Lexi stands and says quickly, "Sorry guys, I've got some packing to do."

Snake looks interested. "Another job?"

"You could say that." She laughs. "I'm heading to Canada to help my friend. She's opening a bakery and I'm happy to help."

Snake laughs out loud. "I can't see you baking cakes, darlin'."

"Maybe not, but that's where I'm heading. I need some space and that is the perfect excuse I needed."

I don't miss the concerned look he throws her way, and for a moment I see the emotion pass between them.

"Do you wanna talk about it, darlin'?"

She shakes her head and sighs. "It's fine. I've been over it with Ryder and Maverick lent me his ear, but I need to change it up a little. This break is just what I need."

Snake nods and then says gently, "Come and find me before you leave. I need to check you're ok."

She smiles and nods before heading off, and as Snake takes her seat, he watches her go with concern.

"Do you know what happened?" I am curious to find out and he sighs heavily.

"I know she struggled on the last job. An innocent woman got killed, and she holds herself responsible for that, especially because the woman had kids."

"That's terrible."

He sighs heavily. "There are many casualties in war, Bonnie, and you can't save them all."

His words remind me I'm one of the lucky ones and I feel a shiver pass through me as I think about the narrow escape I had, resulting in probably the happiest few weeks of my life. Is this something I could get used to, always wondering if he was coming home at the end of a hard day at work? Will he return with the same look that Lexi wears in her eyes and will it destroy me to watch?

As he takes my hand, it chases away the doubts because I'm aware that to gain such riches, always come at a cost. The very thing I love about him is the thing I fear the most and just thinking of him changing a thing, doesn't sit well with me and I already know in my heart I will struggle to leave him if it came to it, so it's lucky we still have some time to come to terms with that.

CHAPTER 28

SNAKE

After we eat, I take Bonnie on a tour of the compound and it feels good having her beside me. I'm keen to show her what could be hers, and I know she's in awe as she stares at the immense space we occupy. It needs to be, given the number of people who live here, and as she gazes in disbelief at the large bar area that takes up a space bigger than most airport lounges, she grips my hand a little tighter. Unusually, it's fairly empty, which I'm glad about because when it's full, it's a lot to take. Luckily, there are only a few random Reapers lounging around playing cards and I head over to the bar, holding her hand carefully.

Millie is playing bartender today and smiles her welcome as we approach.

"Hey, Snake, good to see you back. Good trip?"

From the look in her eyes, she knows exactly what I've been doing and I grin. "The best. This is Bonnie, I could use some help in persuading her to stay."

Millie looks a little shocked and I'm not surprised because I've never shown any interest in one woman before and I laugh softly as she shakes her head and says, "Congratulations—I think."

She laughs to take the sting from her words and looks at Bonnie with a renewed interest, before saying kindly, "Welcome to The Rubicon, honey, it's not as bad as it looks."

Bonnie smiles shyly and I wonder where my feisty woman has gone because she appears way out of her depth here.

Millie says kindly, "Look, anytime you need a friend I'm always happy to oblige. This place takes some getting used to, but when you are, you quickly fall in love with it. Don't be put off by the guys—or the girls, for that matter."

She rolls her eyes and laughs. "We're family and may fight like one from time to time, but we love just as hard."

"I think that's what she's worried about." I laugh softly as Bonnie says loudly, "For fuck's sake, Snake, I can speak for myself, you know."

She turns to Millie and rolls her eyes and says, "Is he always like this?"

"This is him on a good day. What can I say, honey, I'm here if you need me."

Millie laughs and Bonnie joins her and I feel so outnumbered right now.

Feeling irritable, I snap, "What does a guy have to do to get a drink around here?"

Millie shakes her head, "Your usual?"

I nod and she turns to Bonnie, "What can I get you, we have most things?"

"Maybe a beer, thanks."

I knew I loved this girl and as Millie tosses us two beers, I slide my arm around Bonnie and pull her close, loving how she fits by my side. She seems happy to be there and as we lean on the bar; I point out the different guys playing cards and some of the whores who are enjoying a chat in the corner by the door.

By the time we finish our drinks, I'm done with the niceties and growl, "I think I need to show you our room now."

I have an overwhelming urge to be inside her right now and it appears she feels the same because she shivers a little and the flush to her cheeks tells me everything I want to know. The sight of her biting that bottom lip makes me rock hard and despite a few of the guys calling out, I drag her quickly behind me.

I don't even stop to point out the gym, the cinema room, or the games room, before I drag her out to one of the buildings set behind the compound. There are blocks of accommodation for both the Reapers and one for the whores and the married couples live in purpose-built houses not too far away with their families.

Bonnie appears a little overwhelmed by the scale of this operation and I can relate to that—most people are but they don't realize that being a Reaper is a commitment of your soul and to be a Reaper you live like a Reaper, all in and no exceptions.

It's no surprise Lexi needs some time out; she's been working nonstop since she got here and has certainly earned a vacation. That's not unusual. Most of us take a break from time-to-time when it all gets a little too much. I'm sorry though because she would have been a good friend for Bonnie.

We reach my own set of rooms on the top floor and I feel relieved to be home. As second bastard in chief, I chose the best one, and it curls around the corner of the building with views on every side. Floor to ceiling windows let the light in and I've furnished it as well as a single man with no love of interior design can.

It's a large loft style space and Bonnie looks around in awe. "Wow, this is big."

"I can show you big, darlin'."

My balls are aching to be set free, and she glances down and smirks. "I can see."

Suddenly, words no longer count, it's actions we need now and to my surprise Bonnie is first as she shrugs out of her clothes and says impatiently, "I want to see your bedroom—now."

Grinning like a crazy cat, I rid myself of my clothes just as fast and sweep her into my arms and carry her giggling into my room, where the biggest bed awaits looking like a mirage in the desert.

As I lower her onto the crisp white sheets, she sighs and looks so beautiful my breath hitches.

"I love your home, Snake."

Her words hit me hard and I feel a strange emotion grip me at her acceptance of how I live.

"Leaning down, I whisper, "I hope you will call it your home too, Bonnie, please stay with me."

She strokes my face lightly and looks a little wistful. "But how? I need to work; I have a career—a good one. You said yourself the two don't mix, what would I do?"

"Details, darlin', pure fucking details because the only thing that matters is you stay. We can work out the terms and conditions later."

"I get to choose them." She grins impishly and I nod. "Every fucking one of them, except one."

"What's that?"

"That you're my old lady."

"What does that involve?" She smiles with a joy that she's finding hard to contain and I growl, "It means we are together as man and wife. We stay loyal and no one touches you, or me. We commit to spend our lives together and raise a family, here at the Rubicon, surrounded by our Reaper family. I will give you the world, Bonnie, because if you agree, you will already have given me everything I could ever wish for. Please stay, please give this - us a chance because now I've found you, I can't bear the thought of losing you already."

Her eyes glisten with unshed tears, and she leans forward and captures my lips. As they connect, it feels like I'm drowning in emotion and she presses against me and whispers, "I need you inside me, soldier, it's been too long already."

I don't need a second request and slide in, loving how good she feels as she welcomes me inside. It feels so good to be with a woman like Bonnie. The only one I ever want to be inside again and I love how she moans as I rock inside a little piece of heaven. I love watching the pleasure in her eyes as she stares at me deeply, with so much emotion in those beautiful eyes, it's as if we're finally agreeing on something. Her small gasps of pleasure make my heart swell and as the pressure builds, the feelings grow until all that exists is us, doing what comes naturally but it's more than that. It's a union of souls and now all we need is to put the past behind us so we can start fresh —together.

CHAPTER 29

BONNIE

I'm so lost. Lost inside a madness that won't loosen its grip on me. I want him so much I'm prepared to sacrifice everything that went before, but what happens if things don't work out? Where will that leave me, so I enjoy the moment and keep my options open because I need to tread carefully in case I trample on my heart? Self-preservation has always been my motto, and if I was ever in danger, it's now.

Snake and I spend the next two hours in bed and I am happiest here. As long as he's by my side I'm content and reluctantly we dress and decide to head back to the bar for the evening so he can catch up with the Reapers and I can make some new friends as he calls it.

I'm worried about that because most of the women look a little wary of me and as we dress, I ask casually, "Tell me who is married here. All I've met are whores so far and Lexi, of course. What about, Ryder, you said he has a daughter, has he got an old lady?"

He shakes his head. "No, just Cassie, his daughter. The whore who trapped him didn't last long after."

"Why?" I stare at him fearful of the answer and he shrugs.

"She couldn't take his rejection of her and fell into as many other beds as she could, thinking it would make him jealous and he would make her his old lady. When that didn't work, she took to drugs and alcohol and despite everything he did to help her, she ended up dead in a ditch one night."

I stare at him in horror and he sighs heavily. "Ryder carried the guilt around with him; he still does every time he looks into his little girl's eyes. It's made him so protective of her it's not healthy and he will only allow Lou, Brewer's old lady to babysit. She's almost like a second child to them, along with their son Jack. Put Cassie and Jack together and you've got a whole load of trouble, so things aren't working out that well."

"That's terrible, poor Cassie."

Snake laughs out loud. "Reserve jugement 'til you meet her, darlin', she'll have you wrapped around her little finger before you know it."

"How old is she?"

"Four. She's quite a handful, and Ryder doesn't help. He's got her in training and she can fight like the best of them, she's a lot like Lexi, the look of an angel and the soul of a devil."

Laughing, I like the sound of her already and just picturing the big bad president play-fighting with a four-year-old, makes me like him a little more. Then I think about Lexi.

"What's Lexi's story, it sounds interesting?"

Snake grins and finds something very funny. "Lexi is one of a kind. So sweet, innocent and pure on the outside but a demon inside. Most of the men have tried to win her heart, or at least a night in her bed, but she won't even think about it. I've watched her punch a man out cold for laying one hand on her ass and she packs a mighty one, I can tell you that first hand."

"So, you…" I think my face must fall imagining Snake being with any of these women and he shakes his head.

"No, not like that, although I wouldn't have said no. There

are too many willing ones to fall down that rabbit hole, but she's been partnered with me many times in training and doesn't hold back."

"I like Lexi—a lot."

Laughing, I take his hand as we walk from the room and I feel a little better about how things work around here. Unlike the Knights, it appears that these bikers have honor and who wouldn't be impressed with that?

∼

WE SOON REACH the bar and this time it's a different place entirely.

There are more bikers than I've ever seen in one place before, and it's a lot to deal with. They all appear to want a piece of Snake and I expect it's because he's been away and it takes a while to navigate through the crowd but as it clears, I stare with a mixture of fear and interest at the couple watching us approach.

Their president, Ryder King, is sitting on a couch with a beer in one hand and the whore who brought us the drinks in his office on the other. I don't think I've ever seen such a striking couple in my life. Just looking at Ryder makes me want to run and hide because his piercing eyes stare straight down to your soul and strip you inside out. It's as if he knows all your secrets before you do and I feel uncomfortable just imagining what's running through his mind right now and must hesitate a little because Snake grips my hand tighter and drags me along behind him.

"Hey, room for two more."

Ryder nods and I look at the whore draped all over him with interest. To be honest, I'm struggling to remember ever seeing a more beautiful woman than she is. Dark soulful eyes look at me with a hint of suspicion and her long dark hair frames a beautiful face. There's a possessiveness about her that shows as she holds her hand on his arm, and I feel a little sorry for her because he is definitely not as interested in her as she is him.

Just the irritation on his face as he shifts away from her and the fact he isn't touching her in any way tells me that. She is trying to create the appearance they are a couple, but even a blind man could pick up on this situation and I feel sorry for her.

Ryder nods to Snake and says darkly, "I need a word." Snake nods and whispers, "Do you mind, darlin', I haven't had a chance to catch up with Ryder properly yet."

"No, of course, I'll be fine." To be honest, I feel anything but fine and feel a little awkward as I smile at the suspicious whore whose eyes follow Ryder out, even though he never even acknowledged her as he left.

Sighing, she leans back and raises her glass of wine to her lips. "Hi, I'm Kitty."

"Bonnie." It feels a little awkward and then she sighs heavily and shakes her head. "Bastard. Why do I even bother?"

"I take it you're talking about your president."

I grin as she nods. "You must think I'm a fool."

Shaking her head, she sets her glass down and smiles and I am captivated by her because that smile changes her appearance in a heartbeat. "So, you're gonna be Snake's old lady, congratulations."

"For fuck's sake, does everyone know before I've even agreed to anything, what's the matter with that man?"

There's a hint of envy in Kitty's eyes as she smiles sadly. "You know, I'd give anything to be Ryder's old lady. God knows I've tried hard enough, but he's just not interested."

"I'm sorry." I genuinely am because it looks as if Kitty's fighting a losing battle and even she knows it.

"The trouble is, you can't help who you fall in love with and I have—fallen in love for my sins."

"That's sucks."

"It sure does."

She leans forward and whispers, "I just keep on telling myself one day he'll wake up and realize we have a good thing going on. I try to do everything right and yet he doesn't even acknowledge I'm here most of the time. The only interest he shows is when I'm in his bed, and then he heads back to his little girl. You must think I'm an idiot, I know I would."

"Then maybe walk away, don't be available when he calls, play hard to get, it could work."

"It doesn't, he just chooses another warm body to dip into instead. No, I'll just keep on trying the only way I know how because I'm only interested in him. What can I say, I'm a lost cause?"

She sighs and says quickly, "I'm sorry, we need to get you a drink. I'm sure you could use one."

"Thanks."

We head to the bar and I'm glad of the company because it feels a little intimidating, if I'm honest. The guy's interest is hard to dodge, and I feel several eyes boring into my back as I stand waiting. These guys are every girl's fantasy, and I now know why these girls are content to stay here as whores. Surely, it's a dream to have your pick of so many gorgeous men and yet I can only think of one and it physically hurts without him by my side.

The pretty blonde woman who was talking to him earlier is serving behind the bar and she smiles. "Hey, Bonnie, isn't it? I'm Angel, I'm pleased to meet you."

"Hi." I feel a little shy around these women because if the guys are hot, the women are more than a match for them. I wonder why they're here at all but know better than to ask, and as Angel pours me a glass of wine, I listen to them chat.

"So, Kitty, any luck with Ryder tonight. He looked in a shitty mood when I saw him earlier."

"No." Kitty sighs. "I think Cassie was playing him up earlier and you know how he hates being the bad cop where she's concerned. Then there's his sister, she's babysitting tonight, and Ryder hates having to answer to anyone, especially her."

They giggle and I say with interest. "I like the sound of his sister."

Angel nods. "We all adore her because she's the only person I've ever known call Ryder out on his shit. Most of the time he gets away with it, but not with her. She's nosy, irritable and not afraid to speak her mind, in fact a carbon copy of her brother and quite honestly we all wished she lived here full time."

Kitty nods. "She's certainly a force of nature. Then again, so is her brother."

I feel so sorry for the beautiful woman who looks lost in unrequited love, and I wish things were different for her.

Angel says in a low voice, "Have you heard, Lexi's heading off. To Canada I think to stay with a friend. Do you think she'll come back?"

Kitty shakes her head. "I'm not sure. I know she's tired of this shit."

They look at me and Angel says in a low voice. "You see, Bonnie, Lexi is a devil in an angel's dress. She's apple pie on the outside and hot and spicy inside."

"I met her earlier she seems nice."

Kitty nods. "She is, but you must never forget what she does for a living."

"I thought she was a Reaper."

"She is." Angel shakes her head. "Not just any old Reaper either, she's an assassin. An undercover operative who is sent in to kill. It takes a certain kind of woman to do that, and Lexi is better than most. Nobody would ever expect her to be so proficient at what she does, and yet she's a woman and also thinks like one. I know she's been unhappy for a while now and probably needs this break to redefine her goals in life."

I feel a little faint just thinking about what I just heard. An assassin, hell I would normally be investigating someone like that and now I have heard something that shouldn't sit well with me but somehow it does.

I think on the conversation and now I know why Snake was so adamant I couldn't exist in both worlds. He was right. They compromise one another and now I understand it makes my final decision an even harder one.

CHAPTER 30

SNAKE

*R*yder looks pissed, which immediately makes me worried because he isn't one to bring a bad mood into the bar. "What's up?"

He kicks his feet up on his desk and pours us both a couple of whiskies and says darkly, "Cara wants me to let her take care of Cassie."

"As in…"

"Away from here. She told me she could do a better job than me and I wasn't being fair on keeping her here in this environment."

"I'm guessing that didn't sit well with you."

"You're fucking right about that. No, I told her how it is and if she mentions it again, I'm going to stop her seeing her."

"No wonder you're pissed. I'm guessing she told you what she thought about that."

Ryder laughs. "She had a few words to say, but it got me thinking."

"Never a good thing."

He raises his eyes and laughs softly. "You know me too well."

"So, what's your plan?"

"I'm gonna keep a lookout for a nanny. Someone to live in and make my baby into a lady."

To be honest, I'm not sure what to say about that because this is something new. Just thinking of a respectable woman living this life seems like a fairy story, and I raise my glass. "Good luck with that."

He nods. "I'm researching a few agencies and I think I'm going for an older one, you know, someone firm and unshakeable. Someone who takes no shit but treats the child well because there is no way in hell I'm trusting my baby to just anyone. Whoever I find will be the best because Cassie deserves it."

He leans back and raises his glass to his lips. "So, Bonnie, what's the plan?"

"Persuade her I'm everything she ever wanted in life."

"Good luck with that."

Ryder grins and I raise my middle finger. "We both know it's a done deal, I just need her to resolve her past so we can carry on with our future."

"You know she's got a meeting set up back at her department. How do you think she'll handle it?"

His question makes me stop and think for a moment because that's the thing scaring the shit out of me. Just thinking of her leaving and going back to her old life causes a panic inside me I never knew was there. I can't bear the thought of her not by my side, and so I say with determination. "I'm going along for the ride."

Ryder laughs. "I thought as much, but are you sure it's a good idea? I mean, one look at you and there will be questions she may not be able to answer."

"I'll keep out of sight; I just don't want her facing them on her own."

He nods and knocks back his drink and I sigh. "Then I'll

take her to visit her parents. I'm pretty sure that will be an emotional reunion, and I'm guessing her father won't be that happy at the company she's keeping. Tomorrow is set to be a very challenging day."

Reaching out, I grab the bottle and refill our glasses and we stare at each other with desperation. Both of us with shit to deal with that we could sure do without, but so necessary to bring happiness to the ones we love.

~

BONNIE IS QUIET BESIDE ME, and I can feel the tension replacing the air in the car. Today we have ditched the Harley and instead are heading in the escalade toward the town that Bonnie works, or should I say, worked. I'm still not sure what will happen, but I'm quietly confident she'll return with me. I spent most of last night convincing her she's best with me and if anything, she must be feeling mighty sore right about now. I was relentless and so was she. I try to push away the feeling that it was borne out of fear this was our last time. We were both in a dark place last night and I am struggling to understand her thoughts right now.

Bonnie stares out of the window and I can't stop looking at her, which is a problem as I negotiate the traffic because she has scrubbed up like a goddess. Gone are the combats that she had no choice but to wear, and in its place is a respectable skirt with silk blouse and tight-fitting jacket, all courtesy of Lexi. That woman has the sharpest dress sense and I know that Bonnie was grateful for the help. Mind you, Kitty had a different reason in mind in selecting the outfits back at the cabin and ordinarily I would have thanked her for that, but somehow Bonnie doesn't suit being dressed like a whore—she is way better than that.

"I'm nervous, Snake."

Bonnie looks at me and I see the fear in her eyes and I exhale sharply. "Take that fear and use it to your advantage, darlin'. We all fear things in life but don't let it control you. Control the fear and use it to get what you want. Remember, I am by your side—emotionally speaking, of course."

I laugh because Bonnie was adamant I should wait in the car. She's probably right because I'm a scary fucker, I know that and one look at me would have the cops reaching for their guns.

She shifts a little on her seat and says gloomily, "I know you're right, but I can't shake the ball of despair lodged in my heart. It feels as if everything will change after this and I'm struggling to know if it will be for the better."

"In what way?" My voice is hard because if she has fear it's nowhere near as much as I'm carrying around with me right now and I'm almost contemplating taking her back to the cabin until the storm has passed. Just the thought of her changing her mind about returning home with me is likely to send me feral, so I take a deep breath and say evenly, "Nothing will change. You will still be Bonnie and I will still be the man who loves you more than he knew he was capable of."

"You love me." Her voice is soft and wrapped in wonder, and I smile. "Of course, I fucking love you, darlin' and coming from me that's shocking enough. I don't love women, I fuck them but you, I'm interested in way more than that. I feel you, Bonnie, you rip my heart out when you just look at me. You make my breath hitch when you pass by and you make me question every word from my lips in case I upset you in any way. If I don't have you to come home to, I'm not sure I have a home. Does that make sense to you?"

I hate the desperation in my voice and wonder when I got so fucking needy and she rests her hand on my knee and grips it hard, saying softly, "I love you too, Snake."

I almost crash the car and she says as an afterthought, "I just need to figure out a way I can be free to enjoy that."

I'm not sure what the fuck she means by that but that will wait because as I screech into a space in the lot outside the building she worked from, I have to trust that Bonnie will know just what to do once she's inside. Trust is a delicate thing that I am handling carefully right now. One false move and that trust could break, and once it shatters it is difficult to piece back together again. Bonnie holds my heart in her hands and I'm just hoping I get it back in one piece.

This is gonna be the longest hour of my life.

CHAPTER 31

BONNIE

It feels strange to be back. Snake parks up and I look up at the familiar building and picture the usual faces working away inside. Somehow, this time it looks rather less exciting as I contemplate heading inside and my fingers shake as I release the seatbelt and take a deep breath. "So, this is it, wish me luck."

To my surprise, Snake says nothing and just pulls me roughly against him and kisses me as if he's starving for oxygen. It brings tears to my eyes because I know how he's feeling. I feel it too because everything could change inside those walls and I may not like the outcome of this meeting. Then again, it could also decide my future and I wonder if they will make it easy and make my decision for me.

Breaking away, I smile at Snake but have to leave for my own sanity and I don't look back as I slam the car door and head toward the building. My boss, Jefferson Atkins, is waiting and I know will have many questions for me and I'm not sure I can answer him. I know what Snake and Ryder told me to say and their confidence rubbed off on me a little, but now I'm back and facing this on my own, I'm not sure I'm strong enough.

Heading through the door, I move to the reception and say loudly, "Bonnie Anderson to see Jefferson Atkins."

The receptionist consults her computer and then pushes a book across and says in a bored voice, "Sign in and remove the pass. Take a seat over there."

I do as she says with shaking fingers and remove the pass and attach it to a lanyard around my neck.

As I wait, I think on what will happen and I shake inside as I face the prospect of fucking this up and after twenty minutes of frantic thoughts, I am relieved to see a man standing before me, looking at me with interest. "Bonnie?"

I nod and he smiles. "I'm Jack Wheeler, Jefferson has asked me to escort you to the interview room."

My mouth is dry as I stand and I wonder if I'll even reach that room without fainting because I feel so light headed as my guilt rides shotgun on my shoulder because I still can't escape the fact, I killed a man.

The man is silent beside me, which I'm grateful for and I wonder what his role is here because I've never seen him before. Then again, the staff rotation is pretty quick around here and I have been away for a while.

We ride the elevator in silence which only adds to my anxiety and as soon as we step outside, I see the familiar corridor stretching off the interrogation rooms and offices of the defenders of our freedom. The FBI and just seeing the large shield on the wall makes me swallow hard. The mission of the FBI is to protect the American people and uphold the Constitution of the United States. Dealing with domestic and international terrorism, foreign counterintelligence, cybercrime, and more. This was always everything to me. Ever since I learned of its existence, I wanted to be part of it. My father had been and spoke of it with a faraway look of pride in his eyes whenever he remembered the past, and now I'm wondering if it was because of the woman by his side when he was here. Thinking of the Director, my blood runs cold. My father had an affair, and it never stopped. He has been cheating as long as I've been born, I'm in no doubt about that and its emotion that will guide me through this meeting because this is the starter and the one I'm heading to next is definitely the main course.

Jack stands outside an anonymous door and knocks firmly and I swear my knees start shaking and I try to keep it together. Picturing Snake outside gives me a confidence I need right now, and as I head inside, I am surprised to see two other men flanking the one I've come here to see.

"Bonnie."

"Mr. Atkins, sir."

"Jefferson, please." He smiles, which settles my nerves a little and nods toward the men beside him. "Allow me to introduce Scott Taylor and Jarred Harrison. They're from the secret service and are here to find out what you know. Don't be alarmed, it's just part of their investigation."

He points to the chair set out before them and I smile nervously and sit straight backed with my hands in my lap. Outwardly I appear cool, but inside I am shaking like a house in an earthquake.

"Welcome back, Bonnie, we were glad to hear you escaped the explosion."

"Thank you, sir."

If anything, Jefferson seems a little tense and I wonder why and I look at the two men beside him who give nothing away.

"I have the printouts of the information you fed back to us —good job, by the way, it can't have been easy."

"It wasn't."

He nods. "Anyway, the explosion has wrapped things up cleanly and dealt with our problem without any further need for investigation. The facts have been verified, and the case is now closed."

I say nothing but wonder if it's really going to be that easy. Jefferson says calmly, "The reason these gentlemen are here is that you may not know this, but Director Davenport is currently under arrest awaiting trial for her involvement with certain organizations connected to this operation. They want to run over the details with you to confirm what we already know. I'll hand it over to them and then we'll talk about what happens next."

I swallow hard and yet push that thought away and prepare to answer their questions truthfully because this needs to be over before I can face my final decision.

Thirty minutes later and I have answered everything to the best of my ability and they seem satisfied as they stand to leave. Both men seem happy and as they shake my hand, I feel a certain pride at the admiration in their eyes. Jarred takes my hand and smiles. "Thank you, Miss. Anderson, it's doubtful we will need to trouble you again. Good luck, the FBI is lucky to have you."

Scott nods and shakes my hand, smiling warmly. "Enjoy your break, Miss. Anderson, you've earned it."

They leave the room and Jefferson waits for the door to close before he exhales sharply. "I'm sorry about that, Bonnie, they wanted to be present when you arrived in case I put words in your mouth. Good job."

He smiles and shakes his head. "I must say, as operations go, that one was close. You were lucky there was an undercover operative there who got you out. At first, I was pissed, I mean, that was our operation we should have been told, then I learned why and I can't begin to tell you the shit storm that blew up when the facts were revealed. The department is in chaos, as I'm sure you'll understand."

"It was certainly surprising."

I feel more relaxed now the official part appears to be over and Jefferson sighs and lifts his phone. "Jack, can you arrange some refreshment in here, we could sure use something."

He cuts the call and smiles. "So, word is, you've been holed up in a secret house provided by the department your undercover friend was working for. I'm still in the dark about that, so what can you tell me?"

"Not much I'm afraid, sir." He looks at me sharply and I stare back at him with a blank expression. "They never said. I was taken to a cabin somewhere off the radar where I stayed until now. They told me I was to wait it out there until it was safe for me to return. I'm sorry, sir, I wish I could tell you more but I can't."

He looks at me thoughtfully and I'm shaking inside. I can't reveal any information about the Reapers. They told me that at least and so I hold his gaze and as the door opens, he breaks away looking a little disappointed.

"Thanks, Jack."

I look with interest as Jack sets two coffees on the desk and a plate of biscuits and Jefferson says, "That will be all."

Jack looks at me curiously as he nods and leaves the room, and Jefferson leans back and says blankly. "Another recruit learning how it all works. Remember those days, Bonnie, when you have a desire to change the world."

I nod and think back on a time I would have done anything to make a difference and am surprised to find my priorities have shifted a little. Thinking of this department and all that it stands for, nothing has diluted my love of that. Then there're the Reapers living like shadows in the Rubicon. Serving their country in a way that gets them no glory or even acknowledgment. Dealing with the shit the government turns away from and I feel a huge surge of pride as I think about the glorious soldiers who hide behind a mask of fear. Then I think about Snake waiting patiently outside. A menace in every way but worth so much more than any other person here inside these walls.

My heart swells with pride for a man who is so brave and honorable, and as Jefferson speaks, I know my mind is made up already.

"So, take two weeks off, deal with the usual shit that needs taking care of after an operation and report back here for details of your next mission."

Taking a deep breath, I smile and feel the weight of indecision fall from my shoulders as I say lightly, "I'm sorry, sir, I won't be coming back, you have my resignation effective immediately."

He stares at me in shock and I feel as if a huge weight has lifted as my decision claps her hands with joy.

"I see."

He looks at me carefully and then sighs. "It's fine, think on this and we'll leave this conversation in the room until you've had time to think. It's usual to make a rash decision in the aftermath of a difficult assignment. Just think on it, Bonnie, you may change your mind when you've had a little time out."

"It's fine, I've had these past few weeks and I've made my choice."

"Your choice."

He raises his eyes and I smile. "Yes, sir. I will always be grateful for the opportunity, but it's not for me. I know that now, and my heart is no longer in it. I won't change my mind; my decision is final."

If anything, he looks disappointed, but I can tell he accepts my decision and I'm surprised when he stands and holds out his hand, which I shake signifying the end of my career.

"Just for the record." He smiles wistfully. "I'm sorry to see you go. Good agents are hard to find and you never put a foot wrong. Anytime you want to come back, call me, I'll see what I can do."

"Thank you." I smile at him gratefully because I am grateful. I meant every word, but it's what's in my future that sparks the excitement inside me because there was never any doubt that it would always be Snake and I am anxious to get back to him and let him know my decision.

CHAPTER 32

SNAKE

Where is she? I am so wired I can't think about anything other than what's going on inside that building. What if she changes her mind, decides to stay, and I leave this place to take her home? Her home without me in it. I have never been so nervous in my life and I've been in some pretty nerve-wracking situation wondering if I'll make it out alive. But this, this is unfamiliar territory because I have always been in control of my life. Not now though, I stand to lose everything and time is standing still right now because I can't think about anything else but the woman inside that building.

Finally, I see her walking in the sunshine looking like an angel as she heads toward the car with a lightness to her step that gives me a little hope at least.

I don't say a word as she slides into the seat next to me and looks at me with a determination I can't read the meaning of.

"So…"

I almost don't want to hear the next word from her lips and she sighs. "Do you think it's too late to enroll in college this semester?"

She grins, and I think all the air leaves my lungs as I slump back against the seat. "To do what?"

"I've always wanted to study interior design, it was always my second choice and now I've achieved the first one on my list, there's no reason why I can't shift onto the next."

"I think you can do anything you want to, darlin' except one thing."

"What's that?"

I lean closer and wrap my hand around the back of her head, pulling her close to my lips and growl, "Do it without me."

"As if that was ever gonna happen."

Her lips find mine and the relief hits me hard, she's staying and words can't describe how much that means to me. Bonnie has made the decision I never dared hope for, and it's as if everything has slotted into place.

Destiny has left the building her work is done.

Our kiss to cement this deal is long and luxurious, and as she pulls away, I sense the sting in the tale as she sighs. "One hurdle negotiated; the worst is yet to come."

"Your family."

She nods. "I'm not looking forward to this."

I start the engine and program the address into the Sat Nav. "It will be fine. I can wait in the car, or I can come in with you, it's your choice."

Bonnie laughs softly. "No, Snake, from now on we come as a team and if I go anywhere, it's with you beside me. I hope you're ok with that."

"Darlin', I wouldn't have it any other way."

She sighs with satisfaction, making me wonder if we have time to check into a motel or something along the way because I am keen to be naked with this woman as a matter of urgency. Then again, just imagining the emotions that she's about to experience make me feel like the biggest bastard because

Bonnie is about to face the man who has betrayed her trust in the cruelest of ways and I'm not sure how she's gonna deal with that. She may think she's ok but I've seen what happens when feelings get trampled on and Bonnie is going to feel some powerful emotions when she faces her folks, knowing what her father has been keeping from them all these years.

～

IT TAKES around one hour to reach the pretty town Bonnie's folks live in, and as we inch along the street, I picture her childhood. It appears to be a lot like mine and I note the respectable, well-tended properties that mirror many across the country. Decent folks inhabit these houses and live good lives, and I wonder if Bonnie would be happier with a life like this.

Her words are unexpected as she groans. "Seeing this place reminds me why I wanted to leave."

"Why, it looks decent enough?"

"It's sooo boring. Nothing ever happens here because it's not worth the drama of the neighbors gossiping about you. Every family toes the line and lives life by command—how we are told to live it. You know the type of thing, do well at school, find a good respectable job, then the same for a husband or wife. Set up an almost identical home and then reproduce the next generations of zombies who will repeat your mistakes all over again. It's why I joined up, I wanted more than that and I certainly found it."

She laughs and I can't help joining her. Just thinking about how different our lives are to the one she paints an image of would terrify the residents of this respectable neighborhood.

Bonnie suddenly groans and points to a white weather boarded house at the end of the street.

"There it is, home sweet home, it's the one with the flag flying–of course."

She grins, but I can tell she's anxious. The slight wobble to her voice tells me that, and I wonder how this will pan out.

As we pull on the driveway, we're about to find out because the door opens and a woman who looks a lot like Bonnie, minus the bottle red hair, comes running out looking so anxious it settles my heart a little.

Bonnie wrenches open the door and falls into her mother's arms and it brings a lump to my throat seeing how loved she is. It makes me so happy to know she hasn't had pain in her life to this point because just thinking of her hurting is enough to send me wild.

I watch with interest as a man joins them and as he looks past the scene to the car, I see his eyes narrow a little as he realizes this ain't the usual cab company.

Bonnie steps back, and he takes her in his arms and I wonder how she's feeling right now.

Her mom is crying and her father is whispering something in Bonnie's ear that makes her draw back and look over her shoulder at me. The smile on her face brings one to my lips as she waves at me to join them.

It's interesting to watch a person's opinion make their decision for them on the spot because as soon as I step from the car dressed in combats, fuck off boots and a tight tee revealing the ink on my arms, her mom's smile dims and her father looks as if he's just taken a punch to the gut. I'm used to people judging me, hell I would myself and do when I look in the mirror most days, but it doesn't make it any easier to see it every time.

Bonnie smiles which makes me feel warm inside and as she takes my hand, she says happily, "Mom, dad, this is Snake, my boyfriend."

A look passes between us and I feel so proud to be that man, the one who claimed this amazing woman's heart but the look on her parent's faces are not quite so ecstatic as I reach out and grip her father's outstretched hand hard. "Pleased to meet you, sir, ma'am."

They look uneasy and I feel Bonnie tense beside me and I put my arm around her shoulder and pull her close to my side. "You have a beautiful daughter, she's a credit to you."

Bonnie's mom nods and Bonnie says quickly, "Well, are we just going to stand around here all day putting on a show for the neighbors."

Her words have the desired effect and remind her parents of what's at stake, namely their reputation, and they quickly usher us inside.

Bonnie's home inside is as pleasant as out and I take in the clean surfaces and smart furniture, making this a home. Framed photos of Bonnie and her parents are set proudly around the room, and I look like a fish out of water in a place I could never imagine living.

We follow them to the living room and her parents sit nervously facing us, as Bonnie settles beside me and takes my hand.

"So, this is nice."

Bonnie smiles and her parents nod, but there is no sign of joy in their expressions.

"Tell me, Snake, what do you do to earn a living?"

Her father is straight to the point and I say evenly, "Security."

"What type?"

I feel the cop's eyes on me with distrust, and I have to keep on reminding myself I would be far worse than him if any daughter of mine brought a guy home.

"Sort of like private investigation."

"Sort of?" He raises his eyes "It either is, or it isn't."

Bonnie interrupts, "Drop it, dad, Snake works for an organization that takes on jobs requiring confidentiality. Don't make him uncomfortable about that."

Her mom nods and says quickly, "Of course, I'm sure it's, um, very important work."

If she only knew the half of what we do, I'm sure she would be running to hide right now, but I just smile, "Thank you ma'am."

She jumps up, "Where are my manners? I'll grab some coffee, maybe something stronger, um, beer, whiskey…" Her voice trails off as she looks to her husband for support and the look on his face tells me he's way more pissed about this situation than I thought.

Jumping up, I say calmly, "Allow me to help you, Mrs. Anderson, I'm sure Bonnie would like a private word with her father, anyway."

The grateful look Bonnie throws me tells me I am right, and despite the fact her mom looks scared shitless, I guide her gently out of the room.

CHAPTER 33

BONNIE

This is so hard and I'm grateful to Snake for setting up this confrontation because I simply can't bring myself to do it in front of my mom.

As the door closes, dad says roughly, "What are you playing at, who is he?"

"The man I love." He winces as I stare at him with a hard expression and say firmly, "I don't expect you to understand, but I do expect you to accept my choice."

"How can I? He isn't right for you, even a blind man can see that."

"Is that right?" I stare at him with so much disappointment it shocks him a little, I can tell from his eyes.

"Yes, there must be a reason. Is he blackmailing you, hurting you…?"

"Enough!" my voice is louder than I wanted it to be but the frustration is controlling me right now, so I lower my voice and hiss, "You have no right to pass judgment on my choices when your own are so fucked up."

"Bonnie!" His voice is angry but I couldn't care less and the emotion of having to watch my idol fall from his pedestal finally reaches me, as I sob, "How could you?"

"What?" He looks surprised, shocked even, which tells me he doesn't have a clue what I'm talking about, so I just say two words that cause the penny to drop. "Fiona Davenport."

It's as if I've brutally stabbed him and he clutches his chest and gasps, "What about her?"

"You tell me, I mean, you're pretty tight so I'm told and have been for… oh probably my entire life."

"I don't know what you're talking about."

He looks away and the disappointment shatters at my feet at the realization that even now he's going to deny me the truth.

It takes a moment to get my breath back before I say sadly, "Now I know why you always taught me to be strong, it was so I could deal with the pain you inflicted on me."

"What are you talking about?"

He looks genuinely confused and I say roughly, "It's come to my attention that you have been having an affair with Fiona Davenport since before I can walk. Don't bother to deny it because I won't believe you."

He just stares at me as if he's frozen and then says angrily, "You're wrong, I would never cheat on your mother."

For a brief moment, the doubts creep in. Have they got this wrong, did Snake just feed me a line? I have no actual proof of it and he must sense my uncertainty because he hisses, "Get your facts straight. I did have a one-night stand with Fiona, but that was years ago. End of story, nothing more to tell and if your boyfriend…" He looks toward the door in disgust, "tells you otherwise then good choice, Bonnie, you've proved you are a poor judge of character."

I look at him in horror because now I'm unsure. Was Snake telling me the truth? Maybe he wasn't. Perhaps this was all a lie and I've been played for a fool.

My father laughs dully. "I was so proud of you, Bonnie, following in my footsteps, and I could talk of nothing else - now this. You disappear for weeks on 'assignment' and turn up with that beast by your side and tell us he's your boyfriend. What's happened to you, where has your dignity gone? You're better than this, better than him. I'm sorry you won't want to hear what I say, but someone needs to point out you're making a huge mess of your life if you go any further with *him*."

He spits out the final word as if in disgust, and I feel so conflicted right now. Who do I trust, my father who I have always idolized, or Snake, the man I have fallen in love with? For a moment, I flutter between the two and yet there's a look of panic in my father's eyes that offers me a window into his soul. He is looking like a man hanging on to a life belt in fear of drowning. I've seen that look in many men's eyes before and it's usually while they try to talk themselves out of the corner they're backed into. I recognize that look in my father's eyes and the disappointment is so hard to take, it almost drags me under.

Taking a deep breath, I smile sadly, causing him to relax a little as he senses the storm has passed. Then I say in a soft voice laced with disappointment, "Once you have really hurt someone, it will always be behind the smile on their face."

He looks confused and I say angrily, "I believe Snake, dad and do you know why?"

He says nothing and I feel like crying as the hero falls, "Because he has nothing to lose and you have everything. When he told me, I didn't believe a word of it. Then the memories came back and formed a picture I knew was always there. The late nights, the anxiety on mom's face. The sobs I heard late at night when she thought I was sleeping. The unhappiness in her eyes when she looked at you sometimes. There were the times you gave me a ride to school and took a call. The unspoken words spoke louder than the ones that passed your lips and as a child I always knew something was wrong but never understood what? It was always there, the elephant in the room between you and mom that I could never place. Now I know what it was. Has she known about this all my life?"

He almost considers keeping up the pretense, I can see the tussle he's having inside, before he leans back heavily in his seat and puts his head in his hands. "I'm sorry, Bonnie."

I sit frozen in the realization Snake was right. I half hoped he wasn't because I am hating every minute of this. I watch the broken man in front of me wrestle with his demons before he lifts his eyes and stares at me with a thousand apologies inside them.

"I couldn't give her up. She was an exciting part of my life that became like a drug to me. I loved your mom; I still do, but I was *in love* with Fiona. She was edgy, dangerous, and passionate. She was the moment before the ride drops on the rollercoaster and the beauty of the firework. Unpredictable, sexy as hell, and the reckless part of me I had to keep hidden when I became a responsible adult. Then there was you."

"Me?"

It's hard to hear, but every word hardens my heart against him a little more. "How could I leave you? You were—are everything to me and always will be. I promised Fiona that as soon as you were old enough, we would be together."

"Then why didn't you—leave mom when I left home?"

"That's the surprising part of this—when it came to it, I couldn't leave. Where Fiona was the darkest part of me, your mom was the light inside. I love her with the lighter part of my soul, and thinking of leaving her was like a painful kick to my heart."

"But you made her unhappy, I can see that now. Why did you treat her so badly?"

"I tried." He slumps in his seat. "I tried so hard to give Fiona up. I assured your mom I would, over and over again, but I always went back. I couldn't walk away and now I have no choice."

"So, the only reason you're here is because Fiona Davenport is facing prison. Way to go, dad, you get first prize for cowardice. You're not the man I thought you were."

He looks so defeated I think the only thing in my heart right now is pity for him and I say sadly, "Trust takes years to build, seconds to break, and forever to repair. I'm not sure I can give you forever, dad, which is why I'm walking away. You see, when you look at Snake you see the menace and base your opinion of him on that. You take people at face value and don't look inside at their character. I am disappointed in you for many things, but I can never forgive you for that."

"I'm sorry, Bonnie."

He sounds so desperate, like a man scrambling on the edge of the cliff afraid of falling and I say with tears in my words, "Apology accepted, trust denied. You know, dad, you were the single most important man in my life and everything I did was to make you proud. It's just a shame you weren't the man I hoped you were. They say a person grows up the minute they recognize their parents make mistakes. Well, I'm all grown up now daddy, so congratulations on being the one to make that happen. I hope mom can forgive you because if anyone deserves happiness, it's her, so if you'll excuse me, I want to spend some time with the people I love before I head off to my new life, without you in it."

I stand and he blocks my exit saying desperately, "Don't go, Bonnie, we need to talk this through, please let me explain."

He looks so desperate my heart breaks all over again and with a sigh, I nod and return to my seat. "I owe you that at least."

As he begins to excuse his actions, I do my duty and hear him out, wondering what on earth is going to happen next?

CHAPTER 34

SNAKE

*A*pril Anderson is drowning in uncertainty. She is trying so hard to maintain a façade of politeness, but she is struggling—hard. "So, um, Snake, this is unexpected."

"I'm sorry about that, Mrs. Anderson. You must be wondering what's going on."

I lean against the counter and watch her work, and she nods vigorously. "I was a little surprised to see you with Bonnie, we never knew she had a boyfriend."

"She won't for much longer."

I hate the way her shoulders sag with relief and then tense again as soon as I finish my sentence. "I'm marrying your daughter, and I'm guessing you're unhappy about that, but I want to reassure you that I love Bonnie and will always make her my number one priority."

For a moment she seems a little lost for words and then I'm surprised to see her eyes fill with tears and she smiles. "Then how can I object to that? After all, it's all a woman wants, for a man to put them above everything, make them happy and devote their life to them. Promise me one thing though."

"Name it."

"You never cheat on her."

The pain in her eyes hits me hard and I soften my voice a little. "I'm sorry, I'm guessing you talk from experience."

She fixes me with a look laden with pain and right now I fucking hate Bonnie's father. "I was weak, Snake. I allowed something to carry on I should have been stronger to deal with. The sad fact is, I was so afraid of losing John, I turned a blind eye. I didn't realize that the only person who didn't see that was him. He thought he had it all figured out. He thought I believed him. A woman can be a very good actress when she wants to be, but you can't keep up the pretense all your life. I don't want that for Bonnie. I want her to have everything, and a loyal husband is something I want above everything. If you truly love her, make that promise because only then will I give you my blessing."

A look passes between us and I hope she sees my intentions are honorable as I say gruffly, "Loyalty is the character trait I value most. I was raised by a loving family and they taught me well. When I left college, I enlisted in the military and was soon assigned to special forces. That teaches you a lot about loyalty, Mrs. Anderson. It teaches you the value of friendship, love of one's fellow soldiers and love of your country. I am an honorable man and that won't ever change because everything I do is built on that foundation."

"Thank you."

She smiles through her tears and I say gently, "I love your daughter and I fell in love with her the moment I saw her. She is a credit to you, brave, strong, fearless and yet with a personality that is an even match for me. How could I not know that I love her? I never dared hoped to meet a woman like that, but I did and I'm not about to mess that up."

The kettle boils signifying my time is up and she nods. "Then I am more than happy for you both. John may not see it in quite the same way but he'll come around, just give him time."

"I'm sorry, but time is something he's had more than enough of."

"Excuse me." She stares at me in shock and I shake my head. "You may be a victim, Mrs. Anderson, but only until you say 'enough.' Bonnie is a strong woman and I'm guessing it comes from you. Remember, you have to live your best life and not compromise that in any way. Stand strong and fight for your right for respect because you are denying yourself the happiness you deserve."

"What about love, Snake, love has a habit of drawing its own picture? Don't you think I want to walk away, have wanted to several times. It's love that's made me stay because John isn't a bad man, just a misguided one. I know what's happened, I watch the news. Know his, um, mistake is unlikely to be in a position to be a threat to me anymore. Don't get me wrong, I'm sure she is just one in a line, but she has been in that line as long as I have. No, I know when the threat has gone—for now, anyway, and yes, if I see the same pattern forming again, this time I will act. So, everyone deserves another chance at least and in John's case, it's his final one."

"Then I wish you luck, Mrs. Anderson."

"Call me, April, it sounds less formal."

She smiles and I see a great deal of Bonnie in her eyes. They are similar in a lot of ways, and I hope that Bonnie has her mother's soul rather than her father's. I'm guessing she gets her ambition and determination from him. Probably her courage too, but the softness and loyalty in her definitely comes from the woman who appears to have accepted me on promises alone.

Before we can join the others, Bonnie heads into the room and the look on her face tells me our visit is over.

She moves across to her mom and takes her in her arms and

whispers. "We need to leave. I'm sorry it's a flying visit but well, you know."

"I know, honey, believe me, I know."

I watch with a lump in my throat as both women wipe tears from their eyes and Bonnie says softly, "I'll come and visit soon. I'll arrange a lunch date, just us. We have a lot to talk about."

April nods and smiles. "I'm happy for you, Bonnie, your father will come round, leave him to me."

"It doesn't matter, mom." Bonnie looks over at me and smiles. "He is in no position to lecture me on choices. Maybe he should set about practicing what he preaches before telling me how to live. So…"

She laughs and reaches for my hand. "My future beckons, and to be honest, mom, I never knew it would be so exciting."

April walks us out and I'm not surprised that her dad stays hidden inside and as April waves us off, Bonnie leans back and sighs. "It's over, Snake. The path is clear of all obstacles and now we just have to figure out the way from here."

"I love you, Bonnie, did I tell you that?"

"I think you may have said it somewhere back then, but I expect to hear it every day for the rest of my life, or else I may have to kill you—just saying."

She takes my hand and laces our fingers together and now there is nothing that can come between us because Snake and Bonnie have made it—God help us.

EPILOGUE

BONNIE

Cassie is screaming and Jack is banging a stick on the metal watering can and I am out of options. Who knew looking after two kids would be so difficult? Cassie may be an adorable four turning five-year-old but she is her father's daughter and is giving Jack a hard time because he stole her stick. I almost think she's going to wrap it around his head when we hear, "Hey, little lady, is that how a soldier behaves?"

"Daddy!" She screams so hard I think my ear drums shatter, and Snake follows him in and laughs at my expression.

"Hey, baby, cavalries arrived, Lou isn't far behind."

Offering a silent prayer to God, I catch Snake's eye and just the look in his makes me impatient to be out of here already. I just can't get enough of my man, which is a good thing because he's insatiable. It's never enough, and so I'm keen to get back to doing what I love the most—him.

Lou heads into the kitchen and roars, "Jack, put that stick down and come with me. Have I raised you to be disrespectful to a lady?"

Jack hangs his head but I catch a wicked grin on his face

and despite her tone, Lou winks at me as she gathers him in her arms.

Lou and Brewer have become firm friends and I adore them almost as much as I do Snake. I have lost track of how long I've lived here now, but life is good. I enrolled in college and am studying interior design, which I am discovering is a hidden talent. Luckily, I have many rooms to practice on and Snake's credit card has taken a mighty bashing since I moved in. In return, I help out around the Rubicon and babysit the kids and work in the bar. I pull my weight and have settled into life here as if I've always been here.

Angel and Kitty are also firm friends of mine along with Lily, Rock's wife and Millie, another one of the whores. We are a family and it feels good to know that I will always have a home in this amazing place with the love of my life.

Lou says loudly, "Ryder, do you want me to feed Cassie and leave you to finish up."

"Thanks, Lou, is that ok with you, darlin'?"

Cassie squeals with excitement. "Jack, we could play in the treehouse."

I roll my eyes because five minutes ago they were mortal enemies and now all that is forgotten as they leave hand in hand with Lou.

Ryder watches Cassie go with a troubled look and as I catch Snake's eye, he shakes his head, warning me not to go there.

Ryder is a hard man to read and even Snake struggles sometimes and as the door closes, Ryder sighs and heads to the fridge and grabs a beer for each of us.

"Why is it so fucking hard to find a decent nanny in this town?"

We settle down on the couch and Ryder stares at us with a desperate look. "I've exhausted every agency going, but there is nobody suitable. If they are, they take one look at this place and head straight back the way they came. It's a disaster."

Snake nods and I say quickly, "I can help, you know that."

"I know, darlin' but Cassie needs routine, you know how she is. It's an impressionable age and I don't help the situation. She needs a woman's touch."

"What about Kitty?"

I immediately regret raising the subject because Ryder groans. "There is no way in hell I am letting a whore raise my child. Kitty may be willing, but she will always be a whore to me."

I feel myself bristling because Kitty has been so loyal to Ryder. She has her moments, but I know she turns most of the other guys down and only wants him. We all know that, but it appears he doesn't, so I take a chance.

"She loves you; can't you see that?"

"She has no business loving me."

Snake catches my eye and shakes his head, and I share his frustration. Ryder just can't see past her job title because Kitty is as much a whore as I am. She is just in an unfortunate situation and tries so hard it's painful to watch.

Suddenly, Ryder looks up and I can see his mind working as he looks across at Snake.

"I may have a temporary solution though."

"What?" Snake looks as surprised as me, and Ryder shrugs. "Remember Donahue."

"Tyler?"

"Yeah," Ryder looks at me and says, "Tyler Donahue is a man with connections. He arranges women for high profile clients, you know, no questions asked. His parties are by invite only, and sometimes the entertainment is not strictly legal."

I actually feel sick and wonder what the hell this has to do with a nanny for Cassie. "Turns out he overstepped the mark this time and his daddy almost found out."

"His daddy?" I am so confused and Snake laughs. "Chuck Mortimer, billionaire bastard. Tyler Donahue is his cover name, Tyler Mortimer is heir apparent to Mortimer's billions, and if daddy knew his son was breaking free, he would arrange an intervention and bring him back with his tail between his legs. So, what's he got this time?"

"A business deal."

Ryder says darkly, "Apparently, he's not the only Mortimer plotting escape from daddy. Turns out his sister is next in line to uphold the family honor, and daddy Mortimer has arranged a little union with one of his friends."

I can't believe I'm hearing this, and Ryder laughs. "So, Tyler asked me for a favor and it got me thinking. His problem hides out here and Cassie gets her nanny. I get my problem solved and everyone's happy."

"But you don't even know her, what if she's not suitable?" I feel extremely worried about this, but Ryder just shrugs.

"Then she won't make it past the door. No, she arrives next week and so, Bonnie, maybe you could arrange to decorate one of the guest rooms. We have a visitor whether she likes it or not."

"She doesn't know?" Snake laughs hard and Ryder grins. "Now we just have to decide who is gonna break the bad news when she arrives?"

The men laugh, but I feel worried. This is wrong on every level, and at the heart of it is an impressionable little girl. Ryder may think he has found the solution to his problem, but Cassie may think differently. I'm not sure why, but I have a really bad feeling about this and I'm normally not wrong.

CARRY on reading Daddy's Girls. Find out what happens next.

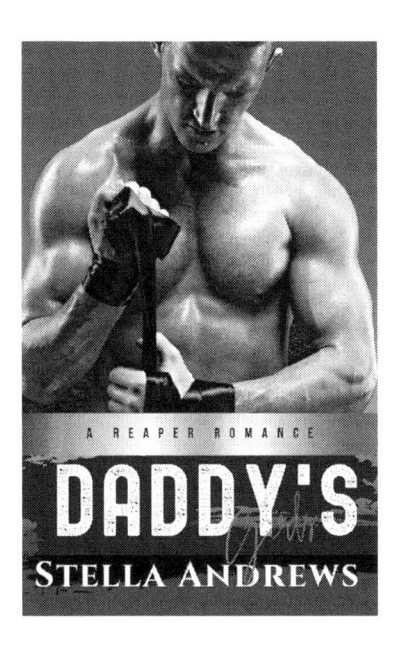

If you want to catch up with Lexi, grab your copy of Break a King – there is really only one woman for the job.

Thank you for reading this story.
If you have enjoyed the fantasy world of this novel, please would you be so kind as to leave a review on Amazon?

Join my closed Facebook Group
Stella's Sexy Readers
Follow me on Instagram
Stay healthy and happy and thanks for reading xx

Carry on reading for more Reaper Romances, Mafia Romance & more.

Remember to grab your free copy of The Highest bidder by visiting stellaandrews.com.

BOOKS BY STELLA ANDREWS

Standalone
The Highest Bidder (Logan & Samantha)
Rocked (Jax & Emily)
Bad Influence (Max & Summer)
Deck the Boss

Twisted Reapers

Daddy's Girls (Ryder & Ashton)
Twisted (Sam & Kitty)
The Billion Dollar baby (Tyler & Sydney)
Bodyguard (Jet & Lucy)
Flash (Flash & Jennifer)
Country Girl (Tyson & Sunny)

The Romanos
The Throne of Pain (Lucian & Riley)
The Throne of Hate (Dante & Isabella)
The Throne of Fear (Romeo & Ivy)
Lorenzo's story is in Broken Beauty

Beauty Series
*Breaking Beauty (Sebastian & Angel) **
Owning Beauty (Tobias & Anastasia)
*Broken Beauty (Maverick & Sophia) **
Completing Beauty – The series

Five Kings

Catch a King (Sawyer & Millie) *

Slade (Slade & Skye)

Steal a King (Lucus & Ella)

Break a King (Hunter & Lexi)

Reasons to sign up to my mailing list.

- A reminder that you can read my books FREE with Kindle Unlimited.
- Receive a monthly newsletter so you don't miss out on any special offers or new releases.
- Links to follow me on Amazon or social media to be kept up to date with new releases.
- Opportunities to read my books before they are even released by joining my team.
- Sneak peeks at new material before anyone else.

stellaandrews.com

Follow me on Amazon

Printed in Great Britain
by Amazon